CHARGE LAND

John Wayne Comunale

Edited by
John Bruni

This book is a work of fiction. Any resemblance to actual events, locales, or persons living or dead is purely coincidental.

Published by Rooster Republic Press LLC

Copyright © John Wayne Comunale
Cover by Nicholas Day, D.F. Noble

All rights reserved. No part of this book may be reproduced or transmitted in any form or by any means, electronic or mechanical, including photocopying, recording, or by any information storage and retrieval system, without the written consent of the publisher, except where permitted by law.
Printed in the USA.

www.roosterrepublicpress.com

Chapter One

Jim Charge was always *in* charge no matter where he went. It wasn't really something he could help as much as that was just how it was. He had a *take-charge* name that was directly followed up by his *take-charge* personality. It was the perfect one-two punch that let anyone he met know that *he* was in charge. Even if *you* happened to be in charge just before you met him, it became quite clear upon his introduction that you had been relieved of your position.

He didn't ask questions. He didn't ask permission, and he never bothered with explaining himself. Not that he had to, anyway. You always took what Jim Charge said as truth, and you couldn't help it. You were compelled to. Jim didn't take it particularly well when anyone denied that his mere presence gave him this power, but the situation was always only temporary. It only took doubters a few minutes in Jim's presence before they realized that he was indeed in charge, and that they actually never were.

I was never confused though, nor did I ever once fancy myself the type of person that would *or* could be in charge. I just wasn't wired that way, you see; I was much more content just being the Number 2 guy. In fact my ultimate goal was to be the greatest Number 2 a Number 1 could ever have, and I was able to achieve that goal the day that Jim Charge walked into the department store and strolled up to my makeup counter. Well, actually I was still in training to work at the makeup counter. Ms. Sandall, who ran the counter, extended my training by two extra weeks, citing that since I was a man I would require the extra training.

It didn't bother me any at all, and I was perfectly fine playing subordinate to Ms. Sandall. Even though I knew the product line inside and out, including having memorized the skin-tone color depth chart, and had personally applied this exact makeup line on the sixteen member cast of the play I worked on last year. The play was about Martians and zombies coming together to restart life on Earth after they had both played a part in destroying it. It was supposed to be a commentary on trade relations with Libya, but nobody got it, and it unfortunately closed the same night it opened. However it was very makeup heavy, which gave me plenty of practice during which to hone my skills, skills that my dried up old twat of a supervisor lacked the capacity to even think of possessing.

Like I said before though, being Number 2 is my thing, and if Ms. Sandall was who I had to be Number 2 to at this point in my life then so be it. All of that changed when Jim Charge showed up, and it sickens me to think that I had settled for such a worthless specimen in Ms. Sandall. Thankfully though, I was spared.

"Hello," said the man I would soon know as Jim Charge.

"Hello sir." I beamed back at him already under his spell. "How can we help you?"

"I'm Jim Charge, and I'm here to take over this makeup counter!"

He slammed a thick, meaty Sasquatch-sized fist down on the counter. It sent a hairline crack we'd been hiding under an old Estee Lauder display spider-webbing out across the glass. One breathless moment later the counter collapsed into giant sharp pieces of broken glass, cheap particleboard and smashed compacts.

"Now see here," crowed Ms. Sandall, "what is the meaning of this? What have you done to my beautiful, beautiful counter?"

"You mean my beautiful, beautiful counter?" Jim asked the question sarcastically as he removed his giant fist from the shattered fragments of what used to be the counter. There was not a scratch on his flawless, well-maintained and obviously moisturized skin.

"Maybe you didn't just hear me." Jim grabbed hold of the trendy scarf Ms. Sandall wore meticulously arranged around her neck despite the weather outside being quite pleasant. "I'm Jim Charge, and *I'm* in charge here now."

With that Jim yanked on the scarf, pulling Ms. Sandall down face first into the broken glass and smashed bits of the counter. She smacked down fast and hard but bounced back up just as quick. What had happened to her face in that brief moment told the short story of how she wasn't quick enough. Hundreds of tiny gashes erupted, pushing thin streams of blood down her face like water falling through a colander. Her mouth opened in such a way that if you were hearing-impaired you would assume she was screaming, but there was no sound coming out. A quick double-take of her gruesome horror show of a face revealed the cause of her silent scream.

A splinter of mirrored glass the size of a butcher knife was stuck through the center of her neck, which prevented the necessary passage of air needed to create sound. Five inches up from the gargantuan gash was a second smaller piece of glass that had perfectly split her right eye. I found this startling yet welcome change of events funny despite the terrifying situation because I didn't much care for Ms. Sandall. Quite frankly I was relieved that I wouldn't have to be a Number 2 to her anymore.

A terrific geyser of gore spewed from her neck wound, flew eight feet across the marble-tiled aisle and hit the spotless glass of the perfume counter with a wet thwack. My eyes followed the blood-spray through the air as I thought how perfect that shade of red would be for a smudge-proof lip liner. It was deeper than *Fireman's Touch* but brighter than *Vampire's Kiss*. Ms. Sandall's blood possessed the perfect balance of violet, orange and yellow to form a shade of red more beautiful than any these eyes had ever seen.

I watched a stream of the brilliant red life-stuff smack against the blinding white of the tiles, and was nearly moved to tears by the magnificence of the contrast. I snapped from the color's hypnotic effect when a giant shiny black wingtip splashed down in the puddle of blood sending tiny spatters of the world's most perfect shade of red out into the air. The shoe that sent hundreds of perfect micro-rubies leaping from the puddle was a wonder worth marveling at in its own right. I could tell the thing was clearly custom for the exquisite attention to detail but also from the sheer size of it. It was the largest shoe I had ever seen in person, and I'd gone to the Ripley's Believe it or Not Museum more than a few times my friend, so you know I know what I'm talking about.

My eyes walked up the leg the shoe was attached to and found it of course belonged to the man who had just conquered our makeup counter, Jim Charge. He was smiling widely using a long shard of broken glass to pick his teeth. He held his other hand out in front of him to inspect the damage punching through multiple layers of glass had done. Surprisingly there was not even a scratch, and his smooth well-manicured hand looked better than ever. Satisfied that his teeth were picked clean, Jim Charge opened his mouth wide like a snake unhooking his jaw and tossed back the piece of glass he had just been using as a toothpick. He chewed it unflinchingly and swallowed down the busted shards like eating glass was a normal part of his diet and made me believe that it should be a part of mine.

Jim swallowed hard, released a satisfying sigh and reached into the pocket of his blazer. Out from it he pulled a cigar so big it must have taken ten Cubans eight days and divine intervention to roll. He put it to his lips and lit it with what I swear was a military grade flamethrower he produced from the same pocket.

"You work for her?" Jim asked. He gestured to the human blood fountain that Ms. Sandall had become as he puffed his cigar to life against the flame.

"No," I said without hesitation. "I work for you."

Jim Charge threw his humongous head back, opened his already obnoxiously large mouth and bellowed out short burst of laughter consisting of nothing more than three resonant and cacophonous ha's. When the third ha was flung from the depth of his barrel-sized chest it hung for a moment before echoing into a thousand tiny versions of itself that reverberated off the marble of the floor and the faux-marble of the ceiling. As if on cue the still standing, still bleeding like a high school volley ball team on a heavy flow day a few months into the season after they've all synced up, Ms. Sandall slammed back down into the smashed counter as the last bit of life escaped from her.

"Get rid of her," barked Jim. He took powerful drag from his cigar.

I didn't even hesitate. Before the last syllable of his order even entered my ear canal, I grabbed the back of Ms. Sandall's purple Chanel suit that she wore every Monday and Thursday. She would wear a different color blouse and change the broach she wore on her lapel to make it seem like she wasn't wearing the same thing, but she wasn't fooling anybody. Ms. Sandall's complete lack of style and attention to detail when it came to her professional appearance were just two of the reasons I was glad not to be her Number 2 anymore. I could already tell this wouldn't be a problem working under Jim Charge.

I grabbed two handfuls of fabric to pick her up by and could tell that the material in my hands was not up to the true quality standard the designer label claimed. This wasn't even a real Chanel suit but some cheap knock-off she probably bought at a weekend bazaar downtown where imitation clothes and handbags are sold exclusively. This angered me even more as I drug her down to the entrance leading back into the mall and promptly chucked her bloody, no style, knock-off brand wearing, piss-poor attitude having body out the door and over the second floor railing. I surprised myself with how far I was actually able to toss her, but I guess my adrenaline had surged amidst my anger over her cheap suit. I heard a few screams come from the lower level of the mall as her body smacked loudly against the linoleum tile of the lower level. It sounded like someone swung a rubber sack of pig fat against a brick wall.

I didn't bother to look down at her as I dusted my hands off and headed back to the makeup counter for further instructions from my new Number 1. By this time, of course, the department store had been whipped into a frenzy over what was happening at the makeup counter, and I was all at once hit by a wave of people running and screaming from the store. The manager of the men's shoe department, Glenn, ran up, grabbed me by my lapels and pulled me close to his face.

"We've got to get out of here," he screamed. "There's a maniac destroying everything in your department! I think he killed Ms. Sandall, and I never had a chance to tell her that I loved her!"

I responded by reeling back and decking him in his stupid face. His nose exploded like a pockmarked, blood filled water balloon as his face contorted into a mask of scared confusion. Glenn was creepy, and it felt good to deck him. He was always skulking around the makeup counter because he was supposedly dating Ms. Sandall, but I didn't buy it. He would come over and hang around the department even on days she had off, or when she was on a break. He never took his break with her because he said they shouldn't advertise their relationship to their coworkers since it could be viewed as a conflict of interest. I didn't know what he was talking about because nobody in the entire store liked Glenn or cared what the hell he did ever. I always suspected he was up to something and never trusted him. Turns out I was right to think so.

"That *maniac* is my Number 1," I said. I grabbed his shirt to pull him closer and hit him again.

The second blow knocked him out cold and his body went slack. He would have hit the ground like a sack of turnips if I hadn't been holding his shirt, which I continued to cling to tightly. I slowly lowered him to the floor as dozens of feet scurried past attached to shaky legs powered by panic to propel the bodies they belonged to in the opposite direction of danger. I bet they wouldn't want to escape if they knew Jim Charge the way that I knew him. I grabbed the limp shoe manager by the collar to drag him back towards the makeup counter and the so-called *maniac*.

I thought Glenn was strange when he used to work in the food court with me before I got the makeup counter gig. He would come skulking around the frozen yogurt place I worked to ask me stupid questions and buy nothing. I took him for a goofy, harmless loner until I quit and started working at the makeup counter only to find out that Glenn had quit his job at The Cookie Shack the very next day. I was even more suspicious when a week later I ran into him in the department store's break room where he told me he was now the manager of the shoe department.

A few days later he somehow tricked that haughty old bitch Ms. Sandall into dating him, and then I couldn't get rid of the creep. It had only been two weeks since he spilled his guts to me about his true intentions, so my disdain for him was still strong. He was waiting for me to come out of the men's room that day and cornered me in the small alcove between the bathroom and the rest of the store.

"Oh, hey Glenn," I said. I tried unsuccessfully to slide past him. He hugged up against the wall so I couldn't get by.

"Look," he started, "we don't have much time, but I have to tell you something."

"Uhhhh, okay. What's up?" Glenn was shaking while thick rows of sweat ran down his face like an avalanche of melted snow in spring.

"Me coming to work here at the same time as you wasn't a coincidence," he sputtered.

"You don't say?"

"Just hear me out. I know that you're a Number 2 and a great one at that. I've known it since I started watching you back in the food court, and even then I knew you were destined to be so much more than that. I think you're wasting your time being a Number 2, especially to that horrid bitch you work for."

"You mean that horrid bitch that is also your girlfriend?"

"That's just part of my . . . well, let's just call it my plan."

"Plan?" I wasn't afraid of Glenn, and he was quite non-threatening in all aspects of his size and demeanor, but I've learned with time that those are the guys you need to look out for. This talk of a "plan" wasn't putting a warm fuzzy feeling in my stomach at the moment.

"Yes," he continued, "my plan to become *your* Number 2. Watching you for all this time has helped me find my true calling, and my plan is to be the best Number 2 I can be with you as my Number 1. All we need to do is get rid of that ol' cooze Sandall, and you can take over her job. Then I'll transfer to the makeup counter and *viola*, our perfect union can begin."

Charge Land

I didn't have to ask what Glenn meant by "get rid" of Ms. Sandall because his tone and inflection told me everything I needed to know. He wasn't talking about just getting her transferred or fired. He had the distinct look in his eye of a man high on his own desperation willing to do whatever it took to achieve his goal, and that included foul play. I didn't like Glenn and, like I said, I wasn't scared of him, but I was careful how I phrased my response so as not to provoke him into causing a scene.

"Glenn," I started, "that's great and all, and I think Ms. Sandall is a total bitch but as her current Number 2 I can't knowingly allow you to sabotage her job. I especially can't let you hurt her either, if that's what you're implying."

"Why not!?" whined Glenn. "We would make a great Number 1 and 2 together. Maybe even the greatest!"

"You clearly don't understand what it takes to be a Number 2," I said, trying to sound calm but stern at the same time, "and besides, I'm not interested in being a Number 1. My destiny is to be the best Number 2 around, and I've worked my whole life to be just that."

"But you don't understand," wailed Glenn. "You and I . . ."

Just then the door to the women's room opened behind us, and Glenn stopped short.

"You and I . . . should get lunch sometime," he continued. "But I can't today since I have plans. Hello, my lovely."

Ms. Sandall had been in the bathroom for the duration of our exchange and stepped between us to plant a wet smooch on Glenn's blistery, cracked lips. She turned around and sneered at me.

"Your break was over two minutes ago," she said. "Get your skinny ass back to the counter and re-alphabetize the lip-liners. Come on honey."

She grabbed Glenn by the arm and led him away. He turned around and mouthed the words *this isn't over* to me before disappearing around the corner. That was the last we spoke of it before all hell broke loose, not that it would matter though. I thought Glenn was an absolute idiot, and he could never be a Number 2, or Number 3 or even a disposable henchman for that matter. Just the very fact that he wanted to be Number 2 to a true Number 2 shows that he has no idea what it is to be a Number 2.

The store's sprinkler system suddenly kicked on, which served only to further fuel the frenzy of the fleeing. The way everyone was freaking out, you would have thought they were being soaked in scalding battery acid rather than tepid, semi-potable city water. The now slick floor made it easier for me to drag the still unconscious Glenn back to the makeup counter and the reason the sprinkler system had been activated. Glenn's limp, lumpy body glided through the quickly pooling water, and the blood freely flowing from his nose left long swooping trails of translucent crimson in the water behind us.

Gray and black plumes of smoke billowed out from behind the half-destroyed cosmetic counter in tremendous clouds of burning poison. Jim Charge stood next to a giant fire puffing out equally black smoke from the colossal stogy between his booming guffaws. From where I stood it was unclear whether the fire or his cigar was causing the majority of the smoke. When I reached the counter I slung the unconscious body of Glenn over the large portion that was recently destroyed by Jim Charge. His flabby, soaking wet, potato sack of a piss-poor excuse for a body was easy for me to pick up and toss despite the weight advantage that he obviously had on me. I guessed it was still the adrenaline coursing through my system that magnified my strength and allowed me to manhandle the overweight shoe department manager, but I also liked to think that I had become imbued with powers on account of pledging my allegiance to Jim Charge.

Glenn skidded over the broken counter and shards of

broken glass left long gashes across his back. The pain was enough to rouse him back into semi-consciousness, and he whimpered pathetically while attempting to curl into the fetal position. I climbed over the broken portion of the counter and stepped on Glenn's chest as I came across to the other side. He let out a dramatic sputtering cough to try and play on our sympathies, but I saw right through it, and aside from that, I didn't give a shit about him either way. Just through his ignorance he disrespected everything that made me who I am.

I walked up to the fire and stood behind Jim, who continued puffing smoke like a freight train. His facial features had arranged themselves to reflect absolute calmness as he stared in serene bliss at dancing flames that wrapped themselves around the black and melted plastic of mannequin parts, which made up the majority of fuel for the fire. A menagerie of generic women's faces permanently affixed with varied degrees of thousand mile stares collapsed into waxy drippings before our eyes. It was absolutely breathtaking. For a moment I had completely tuned out the cacophony of chaos happening all around us as flickering flames transformed these statues into a completely different kind of beautiful. It was Jim who snapped me out of my trance.

"Who's this sack of shit?" Jim pointed the lit end of his cigar in the direction of Glenn's slowly wriggling body.

"His name is Glenn," I said. "He's the manager of the shoe department, and he is a total sack of shit. I punched his lights out and thought maybe we could use him for negotiating purposes. You know, trade him for shit we want from the people who would want him back."

"Didn't you just say he was a sack a shit?" asked Jim.

"Yeah. He's a total sack of shit."

"Then why would anyone *want* him back?"

Jim walked over to Glenn's body, grabbed him by his head with both hands and picked him up. Glenn opened his cloudy, blackened eyes and stared directly into the face of Jim Charge. Jim shook his head and blew a toxically thick amount of cigar smoke in Glenn's face. Jim held Glenn up above and snapped his body forward like he was cracking a whip. Glenn's body detached from his head as if it had been held together with Velcro and flew back across to the other side of the counter. His head remained firmly between the humongous meaty paws of Jim Charge, who smiled and tucked it under his arm.

"I don't need any bargaining chips," he said to me. "I'm Jim Charge."

With that he turned and walked past the fire towards the back of the department, Glenn's head snugly perched in the crook of his arm.

Chapter Two

I left Jim Charge alone for over an hour before deciding to go check on him. A good Number 2 knows that sometimes their Number 1's need time alone, but not too much time. Never too much. I watched mannequins melt as the fire waned from small spurts of baby flame to even smaller embers glowing their last before they slowly turned to petrified ash. The department store was much quieter now as most people had fled. I still heard the occasional far off cry and even what I thought was someone whooping as if they were at a football game, but I wasn't sure if any of it was real or imagined.

The sprinklers had long since shut off, but I could still hear a steady drip from the triggered faucets overhead as they slowly emptied the remains of their reservoir. I walked to the side of the makeup counter that wasn't demolished and climbed up on the wet glass top. I surveyed the portion of the department store I could see from my new vantage point and looked for signs of anyone taking refuge in other departments of the store. I didn't see any people, but I did see a few other small plumes of smoke, which led me to believe that either there were other people holed up in camps amongst the various departments, or a handful of small fires had been set in the chaos of those fleeing the store.

Satisfied that there was no one to be seen, at least for

the moment, I jumped down from my perch and headed in the direction my Number 1 had gone with the head of my nemesis. Towards the back of the department I could see that the door to our storage room had been ripped off the hinges and lay in several pieces a few feet away. Maybelline gift boxes were stacked and arranged in a semi-circle around the opening to the storage room, out from which a soft and tinkling glow emanated. I approached the stacked boxes slowly not wanting to disturb Jim if he was in the middle of something, but to first observe and make a judgment as to if my presence is desired. A good Number 2 knows to never interrupt their Number 1 unless it is a life or death situation, and even then it's not highly recommended.

There were slats of space between the boxes allowing me to see in from several vantage points, and I stepped up to one at my eye-level to take a look. The first thing I saw was Jim Charge from the back, down on his knees and resting on his calves. Even sitting in this position, his stature was a hulking mass of broad-shouldered intimidation. The sheer wideness of his frame blocked my view of what he was kneeling in front of, but I could tell it was the source of the strange glow. I silently shifted to another opening around the side of the makeshift wall in order to see what had captivated the undivided attention of my Number 1.

I put my eye up to the space between the boxes, but then immediately looked away. I wasn't sure what I was seeing at first, but I convinced myself that my initial impression had to have been imagined. I cleared my mind of the unpleasantness before taking another look, only to find out that I was not imagining things after all. Jim Charge was kneeling before a shrine that he had clearly put together in the short time that he had been back here. The base was constructed of mannequin legs that had been snapped off at the knee, leaving the edges sharp and splintered. They had been burned along the edges to form black plastic lesions that kept them stuck together.

Hanging from the jagged broken ends of the legs were tiny gold heart necklaces left over from a Revlon promotion we did four months back. Crudely stacked atop the half-burned, broken legs was a mannequin torso equally mangled in that the head and arms had not been removed properly but snapped off. Even though it was just a mannequin, there was something about the brutality of the implied violence that went into breaking it apart I found unsettling. The torso was from one of our *bustier* mannequins, and on the ample breasts Jim Charge had taken great care in using a combination of powder, blush and micro-concealer to create very life-like nipples.

Broken mannequin fingers of varying sizes were haphazardly melted to the torso up and down both sides. Interestingly enough the fingernails of each one had been immaculately painted with various colors from our Dior spring/summer collection. While all of this was strange, the thing that made it hard to look at was the same thing that made it hard to look away. Smashed onto the neck of the mannequin torso, and held into place by a black and gray striped Calvin Klein necktie, was the head of Glenn with *Russian Red* by MAC smeared across his lips. Strung throughout the entire monstrosity were the Christmas lights we decorated the counter with during the holidays. Their soft glow made the shrine appear all the more haunting.

Glenn's mouth was agape with his tongue hanging out to the side, and his eyes were bulging but not much more than when his head was still attached to his body. Something was off though. Despite Glenn's head being torn from his body, and my being a witness to that, which would in fact make him very much dead, his face seemed to still maintain the qualities of being alive. Perhaps it was a trick of the light? I saw his tongue roll across dry puffy lips while his eyes rolled back and forth, and I realized I wasn't seeing things. Glenn's head was really moving. I stepped back from the hole with the hope of returning my "what the fuck" receptors to some semblance of a base line before looking back in. When I did, I saw the head of Glenn smacking his dark red lips and blinking his eyes.

"Tell me more," said the head of Glenn down to the kneeling Jim Charge. "It sounds like they really fucked you up."

Chapter Three

"So," said the head of Glenn to Jim Charge, "your father really fucked you up good, huh?"

"My father was a great man, and I hated him for it, just as his father was a great man who he also hated because of it. I also hate my grandfather because of his greatness."

"Tell me about it," said the head of Glenn. "Daddy issues are the worst, am I right?"

"This hardly qualifies as *daddy issues*," spat Jim Charge. "The hatred between all Charge men is fueled by our passionate and severe spirit of competition. The hatred we feel for each other is so unique and so powerful that it is the only way we know how to feel. The only reason we love each other is because of the strong hatred that binds us together."

"And all of this is because you guys are locked in some eternal dick-showing contest?"

"Not exactly, although we have compared dick sizes several times and the winner has always been different. With my grandfather and my father and me it's not so much as trying to out-do one another but to create such a legacy that you out-do generations of Charge men not even born yet."

"And you've all been trying to do this? Like, all throughout time?"

"The competition has become especially heated over

the last few decades and has culminated within the rivalry the three of us have cultivated. The things we Charge men have done over the years is nothing short of spectacular."

"Such as?"

"Such as my grandfather single handedly ending World War 2 when he snuck into Hitler's bunker and killed him."

"What?" The head of Glenn looked comical while gasping with the red mess all over his lips. "I never heard that!"

"Well, I'm sure there's a lot of things that you haven't *heard*, but that doesn't make them any less true. My grandfather killed Hitler and ass-fucked Eva Braun after he did it. She liked it, too. Then he ass-fucked Hitler's corpse. She didn't like that so much, but that's Grampa. Always the jokester."

"So what did your dad do that was bigger than that?"

Jim Charge sighed. "My father started the Vietnam War by convincing the people that communism was the superior way to run their country, and that they should resist any and all help from anyone who wanted to change that."

"What? That sounds terrible. Why did he start a senseless war to leave his mark?"

"He only did it to get back at his buddy, Nixon, for welching on a bet they had. Nixon swore it was the CIA who shot Kennedy, but my pops disagreed so they bet a hundred bucks. Well, you can imagine the shock on Nixon's face when my dad pulled out a photo he had taken of himself on the grassy knoll shooting Kennedy. It was the first selfie ever but was never documented for . . . obvious reasons."

"So your dad shot Kennedy and then started a war because someone didn't believe he did it?"

"I guess that's the short version, yes."

"Whoa! Okay, your dad is pretty bad ass."

"Yes . . . yes I know this." Jim Charge slumped and dropped his head to his chest as he said this.

"So . . . what's your plan?" asked Glenn's head. "Surely your master plan isn't to take over the makeup counter at a department store. That sure as shit isn't going to impress a Hitler-killer, or any future Hitler-killers for that matter."

"That is one thing you're right about," said Jim Charge, "but the makeup counter is just the beginning."

I ducked over to another opening hoping to give myself a better view of my Number 1's exchange with the severed head on the shrine, but I stumbled and foolishly grabbed at the Maybelline boxes for support. The whole back section of the makeshift wall came down on top of me bringing Jim Charge to his feet ready for battle.

"It's me, sir. It's just me," I called from beneath the pile. Jim relaxed his posture while carefully knocking the boxes off of me.

I reached my hand through to find Jim's, and he pulled me up easily. As I now stood in the remnants of his barricade face to face once again with my Number 1, I noticed quite a drastic—albeit pleasant—change in his appearance. Jim Charge had applied the highest quality of products from all of our various designer lines to his face to construct the finest makeup job I dare to say that I've ever seen in my entire life. It truly was a thing of beauty to behold.

His skin glowed with healthy freshness from the MAC brand combination foundation and moisturizer, and the Lancôme blush was blended perfectly into the impressive lines of his ultra-high cheekbones. His eyelids were coated in the most meticulous *smoky eye* I've ever seen applied using Dior eye shadow and liner. His lips were the same bright *Russian Red* that I'd spotted on Glenn's head's mouth as well, and I realized all at once how the lipstick came to be applied to Glenn's mouth.

In a word Jim Charge was beautiful. It didn't matter if

he was a man or a woman because he had managed to apply makeup to his face in such a way that he would be perceived as attractive to either sex. I looked up into Jim Charge's flawlessly painted face as he looked down on me smiling wider than he had been when he first arrived.

"Jim?" I said.

"Yes, Number 2?"

"You're beautiful."

"Thank you, Number 2."

"Also, did you kiss Glenn's head on the lips?"

"Yes I did, but that was the only way to reanimate his head so it could be part of the shrine."

"Oh," I said. "Makes sense, I guess."

"Number 2." Jim Charge placed his enormous hands down on top of my shoulders. "Are you ready?"

Being a great Number 2 meant that you were always ready for anything at any time, but it was always good to know what you were specifically supposed to be ready for.

"Ready for what?"

"The two of us are going to take over this great country."

Chapter Four

Jim Charge slammed a flagpole fashioned from broken mannequin arms into the makeup counter, successfully smashing the one piece of unbroken glass left into an explosion of sharp, tiny shards. The flag attached to the top of the thing was clearly homemade and was actually more of a silk pajama top than a flag. Sure, it had been cut up, sewn together and altogether altered in order for it to meet Jim Charge's exact and uncompromising specifics. Luckily, like any good Number 2, I am a jack-of-all-trades and possess very accomplished sewing skills. I can also knit circles around any old lady within a hundred and thirty mile radius, but that's neither here nor there.

Jim had me carefully cut a large C out of the back of a red corduroy jacket, as well as two lightning bolts from the legs of yellow denim jeans. I then used my well-practiced technique to painstakingly stitch the lightning bolts crossed over each other in an 'X' to the makeshift flag. Over the top of the lightning bolts I stitched in the giant red C. It took me a little longer than either Jim or myself wanted it to take, but as I looked up to admire my handiwork flapping in the light breeze blowing from the air conditioner vent I knew it was worth it.

"I hereby seize this makeup counter in the name of me,

Jim Charge, and will from here on out be known as the sovereign nation of Charge Land," bellowed Jim Charge loud enough that anyone who happened to still be on this level of the department store could hear.

My gaze fell from the flag down to Jim's beautiful and immaculate makeup job just as he put his meaty paw up to his forehead in a somber salute. I saluted as well while looking back up at the flag of my new country. Off in the distance I heard what sounded like shelves crashing down and someone screaming, but it seemed so far away I couldn't tell if it was even coming from inside the store so I ignored it.

"Damn fine work, Number 2," said Jim, still saluting. "Damn fine."

"Thank you, sir," I said, also holding my salute. "I take great pride in displaying the skills I've honed that make me a great Number 2. I promise that I won't let you down with anything you may need."

"That's good, Number 2," said Jim, finally lowering his arm to his side and turning to face me, "because we're going to need all the skill we can get to take over the country. Naturally most of the skill will come from me, but I'm sure that along the way you'll have some tricks up your sleeve that may prove useful."

"Yes sir," I said, smiling. "I don't doubt that at all."

A good Number 2 always concedes any and all useful ideas and skills to his Number 1. It was just part of the deal, but with Jim Charge it was different. I knew that out of the two of us, he had skills and power that far surpassed the modest amount that I had to work with. I liked this about Jim Charge very much. As far as I was concerned I hit the jackpot when it came to Number 1's.

"Wow, real impressive guys," came the voice of Glenn's head from the shrine at the back of the department. "You took over the makeup counter of a B-grade department store. I'm sure Charge men for generations will cringe at the very thought of having to top that."

I grabbed a mannequin hand from the pile at my feet and snapped off the ring and middle fingers, leaving the index and pinky still connected, making the hand look like it was giving a hearty satanic salute.

"You want me to go back there and poke his eyes out?" I asked, gesturing to my impromptu weapon.

"No, that won't be necessary," barked Jim. "He doesn't really mean it. He's just a jealous one, but he'll come in handy later."

I searched Jim's face for any sign that he was joking, but I knew a great Number 1 never joked with his Number 2 when killing or maiming was involved, and Jim Charge was a truly great Number 1. I let the broken mannequin hand fall to my feet and wondered just what it was that Jim needed from that annoying, creepy fuck's head anyway? I fought back the twinge of my own jealousy that was trying to manifest itself in the form of a twitch in my right eye.

Jim Charge stood under our flag and looked out upon the rest of the department store, his hands on his hips. Another comically large cigar had appeared in his mouth, and the burning red tip bobbed up and down from him chewing on it. Despite the effort it took to construct the flagpole, and clear away various debris from our new home base, Jim's makeup remained immaculately intact and untouched by sweat or wear and tear. In these few short hours I hadn't seen Jim Charge sweat once, and I imagined it took quite a bit of effort to make that happen.

Jim Charge took a deep breath and puffed his chest out to more than double its already ample size. The seams of his suit began to pop and burst as a large rip tore down the back of his jacket and pants. When he exhaled the now destroyed suit fell from his body in pieces revealing a new suit underneath. This one was an equally high-end, three piece black suit made from the finest material and included a nearly imperceptible silver pinstripe running through it. He stepped out of the tattered remains of his former suit and kicked them to the side as if this were a usual occurrence, so I assumed that it was.

Jim stopped chewing his cigar long enough to draw deeply on it and release a cloud of smoke into the air comparable to exhaust belched from the dual pipes of a Mack truck. Silence mixed with smoke hung between us until the circulating conditioned air moved them both along towards the fragrance counter.

"Sir," I said, "what's our next move?"

"Our next move," he said, not bothering to remove the cigar from his mouth, "is to take over this entire store in the name of Charge Land and our makeup counter."

"But si.," I stepped up next to him to take in his vantage point. "Haven't we done that? I mean, there's no one left here, is there? Haven't we taken the store by default because of that?"

"Boy, are you dense," came the voice of Glenn's head from back where he rested on the shrine. "I can't believe I ever wanted to be your Number 2."

I stifled the urge to run back with my mannequin hand eye-stabber, but Jim Charge put his arm around me and hugged me to his side. He removed the tree branch of a cigar from his mouth and pointed out across the store with it.

"You see that back there?" Jim gestured toward the far back corner of the store with the cherry-red tip of the giant stogy.

He was pointing at the lingerie department. They kept that department tucked way off in the furthest back corner of the store so that you'd only find it if you were looking for it. It was supposed to help keep skeezy perverts from hanging around and freaking out the ladies while they shopped for their unmentionables. I followed the bouncing ball of his burning cigar to see if he was pointing at a specific point or just the whole area in general.

"The lingerie department?" I asked. "Do you need me to get you something from over there? Are we going to relocate Charge Land to back there for a better vantage point?"

"No!" said Jim. "Hell no! This is our home base and I'm damn proud of it."

"Me . . .me, too, sir." I didn't mean to stumble, but Jim squeezed me tight enough to not only force the oxygen from my lungs but from my very blood vessels as well.

"That's where they are," he said.

"Where who is?"

"Those who stayed." His voice fell into a quieter version of itself, yet it still managed to carry the same heft of authority with it. "Those who wish to do us harm and keep us from our goal. The enemy."

I struggled to see just what it was Jim was seeing that told him all these things, but despite my best efforts *and* my perfect 20/20 vision, I saw nothing of the sort. There were wisps of smoke meandering through the racks of candy-striped bras and French-cut panties, but there were the same type of smoke trails lingering throughout the entire store. I wanted to badly ask how he knew, but a good Number 2 never questioned his Number 1 about such things. Instead I slipped from Jim's half-embrace, walked over to the smoldering remains of the fire and plucked out a still burning chunk of mannequin leg.

"I'll go set the whole department on fire then." I held out the makeshift torch like it was a sword I was marching into battle with. "The mixture of cotton and lace will go up in a flash, and anyone who isn't burned alive will come running right to us and to their doom."

"No, no, no," said Jim, turning to face me. "This won't be that simple. Plus if the fire is out of control we risk burning Charge Land down, making the whole thing pointless."

"Yes, sir." I tossed the leg back onto the smoking stack. I felt embarrassed for so impulsively suggesting something that could possibly jeopardize our plan. "I'm sorry, sir."

"No need for the weakness of apology here," said Jim. "In fact I admire your drive and moxy, but this situation will require a more delicate approach."

Jim stopped suddenly and turned in the direction of the lingerie department, again sniffing at the air.

"However," he said turning back to me, "we may not have time for being delicate. They're coming."

Chapter Five

Jim Charge gave me specific instructions to prepare for our impending battle. Surprisingly they did not include gathering weapons or fortifying our precious Charge Land with protective barriers. It seemed that the entirety of our battle plan lay in insults and instigation. Jim requested that I make a second flag from a black triple-XL muumuu from the ladies' sleepwear department and use my sewing skills to attach various fabrics to it so that it said: *Come Get Us You Bunch of Pussies!*

After setting me to my task Jim gathered up an armful of lipsticks, eye shadow and a myriad of different powders and took them all back to his shrine that was once again hidden by newly stacked boxes. I was able to cut all the letters I needed out of brightly colored pink, yellow and orange fabric from old Chanel scarves we had in boxes for a giveaway promo that tanked. I left enough space at the bottom to add my own little touch. I used the deep red Kashmir of a shawl from our lost and found box to add an intimidating skull under the text. I felt it was a nice touch that would show we meant business.

Satisfied with my work I took a moment to admire the quality of my stitching and the attention to detail I gave when cutting out the letters and making sure they lined up legibly on the muumuu. I ran it up the Charge Land pole and stood back to admire it flapping gently in the slipstream current of air being pushed out of the vents. It waved almost perfectly in time with our new nation's flag flying majestically mere inches above it. This was a symbol of our independence as well as a statement of our fearlessness and unwillingness to take shit from anyone dumb enough to stand in our way. With my task now complete I headed to the back of the store for my next set of instructions. I also hoped to coax Jim out to the counter and try not to appear desperate for his approval of my work.

I imagined Jim Charge saying he was proud of me, and that I was far beyond superior to any other Number 2 he'd had or could hope to have. I announced myself as I approached the barrier of boxes between Jim Charge and me. I figured he would be expecting me to come get him once I'd finished for further instructions, but I still called out before barging through the boxes again.

"Sir, the flag is ready for your appro . . . inspection. "

I waited behind the wall of Maybelline boxes for a response that didn't come.

"Sir," I called out again. "Sir, are you . . . uh . . . back there?"

"Hold it, damn it, I said hold it. Stop wiggling around so much."

The voice coming back at me from the other side was the unmistakable gruff baritone of Jim Charge, but I didn't understand what he was talking about. Could he see me? Was I moving about too much unbeknownst to myself?

"What? Wiggling? Sir?"

"Right there, right there. Just hold it there for one more second, and it will all be over."

"Hold what, sir?"

I heard a long, low groan in response and realized that Jim Charge was not talking to me. Against my better judgment, and based solely on the reality that there might be a remote, outside chance that Jim could be in danger, I decided to take a look. I couldn't be sneaky about it this time since when Jim reconstructed the wall he made sure to push all the boxes together eliminating the gaps that I was able to see through earlier. I approached the opening at the side of the wall and slowly peeked inside.

Jim Charge stood in front of his altar with one hand on top of Glenn's severed head, holding it steady while his other hand worked to meticulously apply a new layer of *Russian Red* to his wiggling lips. Clearly the head of Glenn was not happy about what the massive meat-paws of Jim Charge were doing to his face, but he didn't really have much of a choice.

"Ohhhhhhh," I said out loud to myself as it all clicked in my head. "Wiggling."

Jim Charge and Glenn's head both turned to look at me. It was then that I could see the *Russian Red* lips were merely the *coup de grace* of the makeup job that Jim had put on him. His blotchy and sallow complexion was now smooth and glowing thanks to the painstaking application of Lancôme's *Dual Finish* combination foundation and powder along with their *Immanence* tinted moisturizer. Glenn's head's eyes were alive with color thanks to a hearty smattering of MAC brand eye shadow and liner painted on with a master's touch. I never realized Glenn had such high and sharply pronounced cheekbones until I saw them now, underlined by a subtle and wispy application of *Temptu Air Pod* blush.

I realized I had been standing there staring at them staring back at me for nearly thirty seconds now, but the transformation of Glenn's head's face had literally captivated my imagination and completely derailed my train of thought.

"Oh . . .uh," I finally managed, "sorry to interrupt sir, but I'm finished with the flag. What should I start on next?"

Jim Charge returned his attention to putting lipstick on Glenn's head while chewing the end of his cigar.

"Nothing," he said, clearly putting the majority of his focus on his task at hand.

"Nothing?"

"Nothing. Now we wait."

"Wait for what?"

Jim put the finishing touch on Glenn's head's now perfect *Russian Red* colored lips, put the cap back on the lipstick tube and stood back to admire his masterpiece.

"We wait," he said, puffing his giant cigar back to life, "for those pussies to come and get us."

Chapter Six

It was late. I wasn't sure exactly what time because my watch had broken from when I punched Glenn in the face all those times earlier, and there weren't any clocks on the walls in the store. I think it was because they didn't want people to be aware of the passage of time while they were shopping. I think they did some study about the amount of money people will spend in relation to them knowing what time it is or something like that. Same reason why there are no clocks in Vegas.

Either way, I knew it was late because Jim Charge had shed his suit again and was now wearing a sleek, black tuxedo. It was beyond nicer than anything we carried in the department store, and I myself hadn't seen anything so nice outside of a George Clooney, Brad Pitt, Ben Affleck red carpet sandwich of high-fashion one-upmanship. His makeup remained radiant and seemingly unspoiled by the day's rigors. Jim Charge achieved perfectly straight lines and even color distribution with staying power that would take most women five or six monotonous reapplications to pull off.

The two of us stood under both of our new nation's gently waving flags and stared off in the direction of the lingerie department. It was clear to me, being a good Number 2, that Jim Charge was looking at something in particular, whereas I was just staring. I tried to follow Jim's eye-line and match it to my own so I could see exactly what it was that he was looking at, but I couldn't see dick so I stopped trying. As a good Number 2 I understood there were things that my Number 1 could see and do that I was not meant to, so I stood staring, patiently waiting for Jim's next order.

"She's close," said Jim Charge out of nowhere, his deep, megaphonic voice slicing jarringly through the comfortable silence.

"Who?" I finally mustered, almost forgetting I was supposed to answer out loud.

"The one we're waiting for," he said. "The one we need to keep everything moving along."

My first reaction was one of protest, which I internalized so as not to show my jealousness to Jim Charge. Were we really going to bring in somebody else? It was bad enough that we had Glenn's stupid head hanging around for some cryptic reason, but now we were going to have someone else? And a chick at that? Any good Number 2 knows that there's always a chance that your number could be up, literally. If a stronger, and more well-suited Number 2 moves in too close to your Number 1, you could be bumped down to Number 3 or 4 so fast you won't have time to do the math. This new development was most unsettling, but I retained my composure like a good Number 2 does.

"Oh," I said in lackluster response. "What is it exactly that *we* need her to do, because *I* could very well do whatever this thing is, and then we wouldn't even have to wait for—"

I was cut off by the halting stutter of Jim Charge's laughter that seemed to grow louder by ten decibels with each heavy ha he heaved.

"Sorry Number 2," he said, finally breaking his laughter. "This is not a task that you can do for me."

"Are you sure? Because I have a depth of skill in many —"

"She is coming because she will bear my son and

future heir of the all that Charge Land will become."

"Oh," I said, taken aback and mildly butt-hurt. "That sounds like—"

I was cut off again, but this time it was by a high-pitched shrieking that was all of a sudden right on top of us. All at once a torch blazed to life from just in front of the lingerie department and cut through the eerie darkness of the empty department store. I looked up to Jim Charge, who smiled and seemed unaffected, so I held off on starting to panic. When my eyes adjusted to the light of the torch I could see what appeared to be a crudely fashioned catapult made from tied together bras and Spanx stretched to their limit.

The poor excuse for a weapon was aimed directly at Charge Land and was loaded with a ball of tightly packed cotton panties about to be set ablaze. As the torch was lowered to ignite the panty-bundle I was able to see the face of the person who was holding it. It was Missy Cooper, the manager of the entire department store and the origin of the horrible shrieking. She released one final blood-curdling scream that trailed off into maniacal laughter and set the panties ablaze.

John Wayne Comunale

Chapter Seven

I should have known Jim Charge had it all under control, or I at least should have assumed he knew something that I did not know about the impending attack. It turns out both of these things were true, but that didn't stop me from ducking down behind Jim Charge and the makeup counter with my head covered up as soon as that bitch put fire to cotton. Jim Charge didn't move a muscle though. He stood statuesque; his only perceptible movement was the slow and steady bobbing of the cherry on his cigar as he continued to chew on the end. I took what I thought might be my last glimpse of my Number 1 before he was to be pelted with burning undies and then shut my eyes anticipating his painful cries.

A moment later I heard a pop, a snap, a whoosh and a bevy of screams coming not from Jim but from the other side of the store. I finally opened my eyes and stood up to see what Jim Charge already knew was going to happen. The lingerie department was a flaming disaster, not to be confused with the gay chorus ensemble of the same name that performed in the store last Christmas. There were several pillars of flame that were moving around the department smashing into each other, but then I realized that the moving pillars were members of the opposition who had been set aflame when their poorly planned attack backfired.

Apparently when Missy had set the makeshift panty-cannonball ablaze, the fire spread too quickly and ate through the elastic bra straps that were to send the blazing weapon toward Charge Land. When the first straps broke the burning cargo was shot off to either side of the catapult, turning Missy's minions and her home base into a four-alarm failure. If you've never seen a large amount of ladies undergarments dancing themselves into oblivion through a torrid and raging inferno I highly recommend it. It's actually quite beautiful. The fire blazed, lighting the store far brighter than any amount of ultra-violet glass tubes could but then all at once began to dim as the sprinkler system kicked on again for the second time in one day.

Within moments the store was mostly dark again save for fluttering patches of dying embers from frying lace, but even those lasted only as long as the light from a firefly. Besides the steady drip of the sprinklers, the only sound came in the form of moaning death-rattles hacked from the charred lungs of Missy's dead army.

"Well, that was easy," I said. I looked up at Jim Charge expecting to see his exaggerated smile and a hand raised and ready to receive a high-five. This was not the case.

Jim Charge's face was stiff and pensive and in no way was he smiling. He did raise his hand, but not for a high-five. He instead put his finger to his lips signaling for me to be quiet. Shit. A good Number 2 never assumes anything, and here I go assuming away. I felt like a giant jackass and did my best not to let it show as I turned back out towards the lingerie department and struggled to see what it was Jim was seeing through the hedges of thick smoke. A moment later I didn't have to try so hard, because what Jim saw came flying out of the smoke right for us.

To be fair I heard it before I saw it, but the ear-piercing shriek was all the identification I needed. It was Missy Copper but she must have jumped from a rack of ties, or the giant *White Diamonds* display because she was coming down at us from ceiling. I barely had time to notice that she held out a metal shaft from one of the hanging lingerie racks sharpened to a bristly, jagged point because Jim snatched it from the air and crushed it with one hand just as the lethal tip was two inches from my nose. He flung it and Missy, who was still clutching the other end, off the side where she banged hard against the adjacent and already badly damaged fragrance counter. As her head connected with a partially broken pane of glass, she let go of the weaponized panty rack and went limp.

I thought she was done for as Jim Charge snapped the metal rod that had nearly pierced my face moments ago across his knee. He nonchalantly tossed it to the side while puffing madly on his cigar and never taking his eyes off the ragdoll body of Missy Cooper. Any normal person who witnessed this would naturally assume that Missy was dead, but I'd learned my lesson when it came to assumptions and stayed alert and ready to sacrifice myself to save my Number 1 if the situation should arise.

As if on cue Missy's body snapped into motion and she sat up, her mouth a twisted gape of horrific screams. She jumped to her feet, threw her arms out in front of her and she headed for Jim Charge, her hands twisted into beast-like claws. He wasted no time and pounced so fast I thought that he'd teleported. Jim barreled into her like a freight train hitting a fruit fly, and the momentum sent the two of them careening to the opposite side of the store, destroying any and every fixture, counter or shelf that got in the way. Jim Charge hit Missy so hard that I honestly thought she had exploded on impact and was surprised to not find any evidence of her eviscerated corpse splayed across the fragrance counter.

The debris had finally stopped flying and all was still in the store for the moment—but just for that moment—because once it had passed all hell broke loose. The soot-blackened forms of Jim Charge and Missy Cooper sprung from the mess of broken fixtures and burned up shelves locked together in a heated battle. Jim Charge picked up the small-framed department store manager and brought her down across his knee.

Somehow Missy unleashed a savage uppercut on the way down that connected square on the abnormally large,yet perfectly proportioned chin of Jim Charge.

Jim's head snapped back like a toy whose rubber band had been wound too tight and popped. Missy's back cracked hard against Jim's knee, and the snapping of vertebrae sounded like a diesel truck running over a million baby teeth dumped on the highway by an apathetic Tooth Fairy. Jim started falling backwards, his face a frozen cringe trapped in a grimace from the force of the blow. Missy fell the opposite way off of Jim's knee, and the curvature of her broken back made her look like an upside down U that was falling over. They both hit the ground at the same time with a thunderous crash that echoed around the department store for a full thirty seconds before silence reclaimed the space.

"What was that?" called the voice of Glenn's head from the shrine at the back of the department. "What just happened? Did we win?"

"Shhhhhh," I spat over my shoulder in his direction.

"What? Come on man, I can't see shit from way back here."

"Shut the fuck up Glenn!"

"But . . ."

"I said shut the fuck . . ."

The sound of shifting rubble banished silence from the store once again as both combatants emerged from their collective collapse, and now stood two feet from each other locked in a stare-down so intense it caused the temperature of the entire department store to rise exactly eight degrees in an instant. I braced myself for what I believed was going to be a violent and disturbing dismantling of Missy by Jim. I waited for it, and they stared. I waited. They still stared. And then it happened. Jim grabbed Missy's head with both hands and just as I thought he was going to smash it to bits, he pulled her face right up to his, and they kissed.

They kissed long and they kissed hard, and they kissed in ways that I thought were impossible and mostly illegal. When their lip-lock finally ended Jim picked Missy up and slung her over his shoulder like she was a sack of potatoes; he began heading through their path of destruction back towards Charge Land. I immediately tensed up not knowing what it was my Number 1 was doing, or what he might expect of his Number 2 in this particular situation. They were within ten feet, and I was starting to have a panic attack. Jim Charge walked up to me carrying Missy who looked like an undersized fashion accessory against his mammoth frame. He shed the suit he was wearing revealing a three-piece silk pajama suit beneath.

"Number 2," he said, still somehow clutching the cigar between his teeth.

"Yes?"

"Grab Glenn's head and the two of you do a couple laps around the new extended perimeter of Charge Land. Ms. Cooper and I have some fucking to do."

"What?"

"Oh, I'm sorry. We have some *sex* to have."

"Sooooo, we did it? The whole store is Charge Land now? We won?"

"Oh yeah." Jim slapped Missy on the ass. She let out a squeak of laughter that sounded obnoxiously unnatural. "Now grab that head, and give us some privacy. I've got a lineage to further."

John Wayne Comunale

Chapter Eight

It went on for hours. The sound of Jim Charge and Missy Cooper's lovemaking was not unlike how I imagine what rabid wolverines tied in a sack and put in a dryer along with a sock full of quarters would sound. There was just so much screeching, pounding and jangling. So much jangling. I walked the perimeter of the store with Glenn's head twelve times before we decided that they weren't going to be done anytime soon, and we thought we'd explore some of the other departments.

I also took the liberty, being a good Number 2, to lower and lock the gates that granted access to Charge Land from the rest of the mall as well as outside. I used the backsides of two oversized Guess jeans display posters and a fresh tube of *Russian Red* to create signs that I pressed up against the gates so they could be clearly seen from the outside. They said, "Welcome to Charge Land. Please Fuck OFF!" It wasn't as poetic as I would have liked, but I had limited space, and I think it conveyed the sentiment well enough.

"Man, they sure have been boning for a long time," said the head of Glenn. "Does it make you jealous that your precious Number 1 favors a piece of ass above his piss-poor excuse for a Number 2?"

I had been cradling Glenn's head in the crook of my arm as we walked, and I dropped him face first and kicked him like a soccer ball back up into my hands. He yelped as I caught him, then I flipped him back around to face me and slapped him a couple times.

"A good Number 2," I said between slaps, "knows that the relationship between his Number 1 and him, and his Number 1 and any of their sexual suitors is completely separate and different. This is why you would make a horrible Number 2."

I dropped the head again this time kicking him around a few times like an oversized hacky sack. Satisfied that I'd gotten my point across, I tucked Glenn's head back into my arm and continued making our way to the sporting goods department.

"You know," said Glenn's head, "you're a real asshole!"

I held the head out in front of me and feigned dropping it again. Glenn closed his eyes and bit his lip in anticipation of the impending kick, but I caught him at the last second and tucked him back where he was.

"Such an asshole," he muttered under his breath. I smiled, pretending I didn't hear him.

We passed the smoldering piles of ash that had been the reluctant members of Missy's army, but aside from them there was no sign of anyone else in the department store. Sure, the place was huge and someone could have been hiding in any number of places, but something told me that Jim Charge, Missy, Glenn's head and myself were the only people (so to speak) left in the store. The lingerie department was a complete disaster with nothing worth salvaging, so we hooked on past to the far opposite corner which housed the sporting goods department.

"What are we doing here?" asked Glenn's head. "You don't strike me as a sportsman."

I took three running steps to the portable basketball goal that was set up against the wall, jumped and executed a layup with Glenn's head so perfectly that Larry Bird himself would be proud of my form. Glenn's head smacked against the backboard at the top right corner of the red square and fell through the net with a swoosh followed directly by the hollow thunk of it hitting the floor.

"Wooo!" I yelled. "And one! One of my old Number 1's was a basketball nut that could only relieve stress by shooting hoops and playing pick-up games with strangers. I played *a lot* of basketball during that time in my life."

I bent over and picked up Glenn's head that had of course landed face first on the cold tile below.

"Man, you truly are an asshole, you know that?"

Glenn now had the puffy, purple start of what I was sure would bloom into a terrific shiner, along with a thin rivulet of blood dripping from his nose.

"Yup, I do. We're gonna' have to get Jim to redo your makeup when we get back. I know he's good and all, but he's going to have to perform a miracle to cover that black eye."

"Shit man, are you serious? How bad does it look? My face is all I have to work with now, so I'd appreciate it if you would stop kicking me around and using me as sports equipment."

"Well, I would appreciate it if you would die like any good and decent severed head would do instead of calling me an asshole every five minutes."

"Hey, I can't help that, all right?" squawked Glenn's head. "I don't like it any more than you do, but you heard Jim. He needs me for some part of his grand plan."

"I wish he would hurry up and use you for whatever he needs so I can be rid of you already."

"Don't be jealous because your precious Number 1 needs something done that he knows you are clearly incapable of doing. I'm sure whatever it is, it will require me sticking around quite a bit longer than you'd like."

"How do you know that?"

"It's just a feeling I have." Glenn's head smirked up at me as I held him tight by the ears.

I hated to think that Glenn's head might be right, and I didn't even want to start thinking about what it was that this obnoxious severed head could do that I couldn't.

"Oh hey," I said, smiling and pointing across the department, "is that one of those new portable bowling lanes? I'd sure like to try that thing out."

"Wait, wait, no," said Glenn's head as I pulled back my arm in preparation to chuck him in the direction of the pins.

Just then a tremendous roar mixed with a skin-crawling, nearly inaudible high-pitched squealing came from the direction of the original Charge Land. The sound startled me, and Glenn's head slipped from my hold and flew off right into a display of jockstraps and sports bras causing all the shelves to collapse down onto him. His screams were muted from the XXXL jockstraps that now buried him.

Then, it was quiet. There were no more grunts, screeches or jangles, which led me to believe that the horrendous sound we'd just heard was that of my Number 1 and his lady-faire climaxing. As disturbing as it was for me to associate that sound with sexual pleasure, I silently rejoiced because it meant we could head back to the Charge Land home base for further instructions. I raced over to the collapsed shelves and started pitching handfuls of bras and jock straps behind me until I found Glenn's head deep in the mess. His other eye was now blackened as well, and the blood from his nose had far surpassed a trickle and bathed the entire lower half of his face in red viscous.

"Shit! Shit! Shit! You really are . . ."

"Yeah, yeah, I know," I said, wiping his face clean with an extra-large sports bra. "I'm an asshole. Now pipe down and let's head back over there."

Satisfied that I had cleaned him up as best I could, I grabbed a ball bag made of mesh netting, threw Glenn's head inside and slung it over my shoulder.

"Real nice man, thanks a lot," croaked Glenn's head.

"Don't be such a pussy," I said to him. "You're bleeding like a stuck pig, and I'm not getting blood all over my shirt."

"Whatever."

The short trip back was spent in silence, but I could feel Glenn squirm in the bag against my back. I imagined the prick was doing his best to rub as much blood and snot into my shirt as possible the entire time. As we approached the makeup counter, the original home base of Charge Land, the place looked unrecognizable. I mean, it was majorly fucked before we left what with all the smashing and the breaking and the bonfire, but that was mere cosmetic damage compared to this. Not one piece of the counter stood and was now flattened into a mix of shattered glass, twisted metal framing and nearly disintegrated particle board all covered in a drippy layer of age-defying moisturizer and what I could only guess was jizz.

The only thing that hadn't been destroyed was the flagpole made of melted mannequin parts and the Charge Land flag. The other flag I had made per Jim's request to call out our enemy was noticeably missing.

"Jesus Christ," I said, surveying the damage.

"What is it? Turn around I can't see," shouted Glenn's head.

"Hold on," I said. "Just shut up for a second."

Thoughts of the worst possible scenarios began playing through my mind. Maybe Jim and Missy were not boning after all but instead engaged in fierce and extreme battle. A battle that destroyed Charge Land. A battle that quite possibly destroyed Jim Charge as well. My palms started to sweat, and my mouth went dry as tiny panic bubbles worked their way up from my stomach to tickle the back of my throat. If Jim Charge had indeed been vanquished by that cunt Missy Cooper, then where did that leave me? Was I now obligated by some code of battle to serve as

Number 2 to Missy, or would I be instead forced into being a Number 1 with Glenn's head as my Number 2? Neither option looked good to me.

"Would you just tell me what in the hell is going on, for Christ's sake? I mean, it's bad enough that you put me in a bag, but . . . "

I'd had enough of Glenn's head's mouth, and without thinking about it I reflexively threw the bag right into the smoking pit that was Charge Land.

"See for yourself you whiny prick," I said as Glenn's head disappeared in the smoke and rattled around amongst the wreckage.

For a moment, and I mean a very small, nearly microscopic moment, I felt a pang of dread and remorse for throwing what could be the last and only *friend* I had left. The feeling quickly vanished when I heard Glenn's head call out from the rubble.

"Shit man, that really hurt, you fuck. It's bad enough you gave me two black eyes, but I'm pretty sure my nose is broken now, and . . . Jesus what is all this sticky goo all over the place? I'm covered in it."

I laughed out loud as I ventured into the ruins of the old makeup counter towards where I guessed Glenn's head had landed. The first step I took past where the counter once stood could very well have been my last as my foot landed in a puddle of this mystery goo that seemed to cover everything. My front foot slid out fast from under me while my back one stayed planted. Just as I was about to execute a Van Damme-style split a la *Blood Sport,* my ass hit something that stopped me from going all the way down.

Whatever it was had at the very least saved me from a nasty groin pull, which I was thankful for until I felt the thing move. Not move around exactly, but it was more like it was breathing. I could feel the rush of warm air through my slacks against my taint and asshole very well due to the fact that I wasn't—and never do—wear undies.

The breathing turned quickly into vibrations, which turned even quicker into sounds until I realized just what exactly had (somewhat) broken my fall. I had landed smack dab onto Glenn's head's face, which was now thoroughly and exclusively nuzzled in the crevice between my ass and balls.

"Hmmmmphhhhhh," came the muffled voice of Glenn's head.

I grabbed a nearby piece of debris and began to pull myself up, but not too quickly. I wanted to make sure Glenn didn't forget the smell of my soggy bottom pit for some time to come. I finally pulled myself off of him and to my feet.

"Oh god, oh god, oh god," said Glenn's head. "What the hell was that? Do you wash your ass with spoiled milk and someone else's dirty ass? If I could puke I'm sure I'd be doing it all over the place."

I reached down, grabbed the mesh bag that still held the head captive and held it out in front of me.

"Oh hey Glenn," I said, acting aloof. "Man, you really saved me there. I thought I was gonna' bust my ass and break a leg or even worse. I owe you one buddy."

My tone dripped so saccharinely sweet with sarcasm that Glenn's head could only cough and curse at me in response. I pulled the drawstrings of the goo-soaked bag to open it and retrieved Glenn's head from his netted prison. The crisscross pattern of the mesh sack had cut its way into Glenn's head's skin making it look like he had been smacked several times with a hot waffle iron. The sight of him made me smile.

"Oh man," said Glenn's head, spitting out a messy, dripping loogie. "My face really hurts."

The sight of it dangling from his lip made me wonder if some of the mystery goo that surrounded us had somehow made its way up the hole of his severed esophagus and come out his mouth. (No pun intended.)

"Where does it hurt?" I asked, playing dumb.

"I don't know!" he shouted back at me. "It hurts like, all over. Do I have any marks on my face anywhere?"

I held his head up to pretend to get a better look in the light.

"Nope," I said confidently. "You're lookin' good man. Ship shape."

"Really? You don't see anything? Because it hurts like a son of a bitch."

"No, no, no," I said, rotating his head in the small amount of light, pretending to check all angles. "I'm not seeing anything out of the ordinary."

I was having so much fun fucking with Glenn's head, literally, that I nearly forgot about our situation and the destruction around us. I suddenly snapped back into the moment when I heard what sounded like a bear giving birth with a bullhorn to its mouth. It came from the back of the department where Jim's shrine had been. Our eyes cut to the direction of the sound, but all we saw was the supply closet now completely covered up by foam tiles, ceiling beams and silver pieces of HVAC that had fallen during the fight.

A moment later the sound came again and we traded a quick glance with each other before turning back to where it came from. The sound came again, louder this time, followed by an explosion of debris from the supply closet. I dropped Glenn's head, although not on purpose, and ducked down to avoid being smacked across the face with a flying air-vent grate.

"You fucker," moaned Glenn's head as he bounced off the tile face first.

I reached out and grabbed him just in case we had to make a run for it, but as the dust began to settle the recognizably large silhouette of Jim Charge emerged from the supply closet followed closely behind by Missy Cooper. Jim Charge had shed his suit once again and was now clad in a classic all-white tuxedo that he pulled off remarkably. Missy was wearing a silky leopard-print negligée that was at least three sizes too big. It had to have been the only piece of lingerie that survived the blaze of her botched attack.

"Gentlemen," came the booming voice of Jim Charge through the smoke. He snatched up Missy Cooper and held her in his arms out in front of him. "Behold, your queen!"

John Wayne Comunale

Chapter Nine

I tried my best to hide the disappointment, anger and resentment I was all at once feeling although apparently not as well as I'd thought. Glenn's head seemed to pick up on the subtle change in my tone and body language after Jim Charge had announced Missy as his queen. The initial blow wasn't too hard to stomach. After all, Number 1's almost always find a steady sexual partner for varying lengths of time, which is nothing a good Number 2 ever has to worry about. Sure, you did hear about jealous, self-centered Jezebels convincing their counterpart to ditch their Number 2 in order to greedily usurp all the attention for themselves, but I didn't feel like I had to worry about that with Jim Charge.

What did worry me, though, was just after Jim made the declaration of their relationship status; he quickly followed it up by also announcing that she was pregnant with his son. As we stared back at the towering marvel of a man he continued explaining that Charge men knew how to impregnate women, and that they never missed their mark. He also told us that the gestation time for Charge men was very short, hence the oversized negligée he'd stuck Missy in and the reason for our current assignment.

Jim sent Glenn's head and I to the children's department of the store to scrounge up whatever supplies we could find for when the Charge child was born.

Apparently it was a lot sooner than we thought because Jim told us to be back in no more than thirty minutes. He said that then it would be time to execute the next vital step of our plan. As we traversed through the wet and blackened rubble, I did my best not to think about what the future held for Jim Charge and me. Having a girlfriend is one thing and not too big of a threat for a good Number 2, but a kid is a challenge for even the greatest of Number 2's to compete with.

"Why are you so down in the dumps?" asked Glenn's head. I was absentmindedly clutching him like a rookie running back with a fumbling problem. "I'm sure that after Jim fires you as his Number 2, he'll give you a job changing his kid's shitty drawers. Maybe he'll hire you to pump rancid milk out of those worthless, fried-egg-on-a-nail, sorry excuse for a set of titties on his new *Queen* Missy? After that maybe Jim could have you drink the milk yourself and throw it up into the kid's mouth so you can feed him all baby-bird style or something?"

I suppressed the urge to chuck Glenn's head across the store, not wanting to risk possibly upsetting my Number 1 during a crucial time such as this. Jim told me specifically that having Glenn's head around somehow fit into his plan, and a good Number 2 never interferes with any plans his Number 1 had regardless of whether or not you felt conflicted.

"Oh, I don't know," I said, looking down at Glenn's head in my arms. "I think a job like sucking milk out of the horrifyingly sickening and unsexy breasts of their leader's lover would be far more suited for a severed head with a hose jammed up its neck-hole. What do you think?"

Glenn's head mumbled to himself quietly and chose not to engage me in further conversation for the rest of the walk. I checked the timer I had set on my watch to find that only four of the thirty minutes had passed. I had at least twenty-six possible minutes to spend with this stupid head and then hopefully Jim Charge would throw it into a volcano or skull-fuck it to death or whatever he needs to do to further his plan. A designer brand, over-priced, souped-up stroller blocked the aisle fifteen feet in front of us, so I reared back and lobbed Glenn's head towards it underhand softball pitch style. Glenn's head had no idea what I was throwing him at, just that I had thrown him and he was not happy.

"Fuck, fuck, fuck, fuck, fuck, fuck," cried Glenn's head as it sailed end over end towards the fancy stroller. "Yoooooooooouuuuuuuu!"

Glenn's head hit the Tempur-Pedic cushioned, mink-lined interior of the stroller and was rolled up in the matching goose-down comforter with silk duvet cover, both of which are sold separately, of course. A moment later I was grasping the handles of the stroller and staring down at a face only a mother could love.

"What's wrong Glenn?" I teased. "Baby want his bottle?"

"Can it," said Glenn's head, "and get me out of this fucking blanket."

"Baby doesn't wike his wittle bwanky wanky? Here, let mommy fix that for baby."

I reached down, pulled the blanket up over Glenn's head's mouth and tucked the excess down into the sides of the stroller making it impossible for him to move or talk.

"Grhmmmphhhh," tried Glenn's head through the blanket.

"There, there dear. Just quiet down, and everything will be fine. Now let's get whatever we can find that's still worth a damn in this department and take it back to Jim."

As I speedily pushed the stroller Glenn's head moaned for a little while longer before finally quieting down completely. When I threw in an Elmo onesie and six random diapers I found that hadn't gotten wet I saw

Glenn's head had actually dozed off, and I placed the items gingerly in the stroller so as not to wake him. I needed a break from his smart mouth and all his talk about Jim Charge demoting me to his diaper changing, tit-sucking nanny.

While this was an all too accurate and realistic possibility, it was one I did not want to dwell on. I had only just become Jim Charge's Number 2, and I'd be damned if I wasn't going to do all that I could to stay. I would show him I was a great and indispensable Number 2 by doing whatever it took to get his plan launched. I moved through the entire department quickly and silently like some kind of baby-stuff-fetching ninja who doesn't want to wake up the severed head in the stroller that he's pushing around. I grabbed what I could, but the pickings were slim. I managed to find a blanket, four more diapers and a See and Say that only spoke Spanish. The rest was wet, covered in soot or both.

I was confident that Jim Charge would be able to make do with the things that I had scavenged, and seeing as the half hour time limit in which I was allotted to procure these items was quickly coming to a close, this was as good as it was going to get. I pointed the stroller in the direction of Charge Land and began to quickly make my way back, being careful to navigate the rubble in such a way that I did not wake Glenn's head. I neared the Charge Land flag still flying in all its glory from our homemade and unintentionally macabre flagpole of mannequin parts, hoping that the next set of orders I received from my Number 1 would include skewering Glenn's head on a sharpened post. I could already make out the grand silhouette of Jim Charge standing proudly beneath the long and lazy flaps of the waving flag.

I quickened my pace, not caring if I woke Glenn's head in my haste to return home to Jim Charge. I could see him clearly now, noticing that his suit had transformed once again and was now a dark gray three-piece tweed number with a day-glow yellow tie that popped so hard I thought it might burn my retinas out. A bold and daring combination, this much is true, but there didn't seem to be any look that Jim Charge couldn't pull off with confidence and undeniable swagger. I secretly wished I had the exact same suit even though I loathe Number 2's who dress like their Number 1's. It's just pathetic.

My smile drooped and eventually faded completely when I noticed Jim's arm wrapped tightly around Missy, holding her as close to his side as possible. She was still wearing the same oversized negligée from when I saw her thirty minutes ago, only now it wasn't quite as oversized. I wouldn't have believed it if I wasn't seeing it, but Missy Cooper was most definitely sporting a baby-bump. It wasn't super-huge, but it was there and it was noticeable. Heavy clouds of thick white smoke billowed in steady puffs from the cigar that still dangled from Jim Charge's mouth as he motioned for me to hurry with the arm that wasn't currently pinning Missy Cooper to his side.

"What's . . . what's going on now?" asked Glenn's head from the bouncing stroller. All the shaking had freed him from his blanket bonds allowing him to talk but still not see.

"We're going to find out the next part of the plan, which hopefully includes getting rid of you," I launched down at him while breaking out into a full on run. "Now do me a favor and just shut the hell up!"

I purposely rammed the stroller into a rack of women's pantsuits causing Glenn's head to roll onto his face and get stuck against the side, which successfully eliminated his ability to speak once again. Reaching my destination I slowed to a stop and caught my breath while standing in the colossal shadow of my Number 1. I was finally close enough to see that his makeup had been completely redone, and his sheer and perfect beauty stunned me. The painting on his face was simpler overall but stood out boldly in all the right spots. His impossibly high cheekbones appeared even impossibly higher, and his eyebrows were perfection in arch form. His lips were shiny *Bubble Gum Pink* by MAC and nearly drew attention completely away from the faux mole he had added above the left side of his lip.

"Welcome back Number 2," said Jim, bearing his cheesy trademark smile.

"Thank you sir," I said, doing my best to still catch my breath. "I brought you some things for the . . ."

"Do you still have the head?" Jim asked, cutting me off but then quickly erasing his curtness with another smile.

"Head? Oh, Glenn's head. Yeah, I still have him in here." I reached in the stroller and pulled Glenn's head out from under a pile of diapers and assorted other semi-useless baby crap. "Here. Here, take him. That is unless you want me to ram him through a sharp spike somewhere?"

"No, no, no," said Jim Charge. He took Glenn's head from me, holding it like a tiny pellet in his massive mitt. "I finally need this little guy."

Jim opened his mouth wide and let his cigar fall to the ground. He opened his mouth as wide as it would go, and then he opened it even wider. It was as if his head were actually growing more bone and tissue right before my eyes for the express purpose of allowing him to open his mouth so wide. Then, just when I thought the top of Jim's head was going to fall backwards off the rest of his body, he bent forward and closed his mouth with Missy's head completely inside. I heard a snap, a tear, another tear and then a slow rip before the pregnant body of Missy Cooper was free from my Number 1's mandibles. However she was now just a pregnant body since her recently separated head was still inside Jim Charge's mouth.

The body took a few slow steps away as its hands clutched madly for a head that wasn't there anymore. Jim Charge chewed a surprisingly few amount of times before swallowing the head down. A beat later a geyser of blood erupted from Missy's headless neck hole, but before the blood spray even had a chance to hit the ceiling, Jim Charge slammed Glenn's head down over the gaping wound and twisted it on. After several solid revolutions there was a click, and Glenn's head snapped into place. Missy's body held its hands up in front of Glenn's head's face as it took them both a second to realize they were now one.

"Holy shit," said Glenn's head, using Missy's hands to feel his own face. "I have a body again! I have a body again!"

Glenn's hands moved down his face to clutch the mildly swollen but still unimpressive breasts of his new found body.

"I have tits," said Glenn, groping them suggestively. "Holy shit on a shingle, I have me some titties! Wait, wait, wait. Ahh shit. This means I don't have a dick doesn't it?"

John Wayne Comunale

Chapter Ten

Jim Charge shed the tweed suit he was wearing when I walked up to him, and in its place sprouted a deep red velvet suit with a long jacket and a fitted black collared shirt, *sans* tie, left open at the neck. It was virtually impossible for there to be a look he couldn't pull off without having to put any effort into it. I mean, I'm his Number 2 and, if asked prior to, even I would have advised against such a suit but actually seeing it tells me that I would have been absolutely wrong. He was a stunning specimen of a person possessing a limitless amount of charm and confidence that all Charge men must be made of. I imagine they passed it to each other through some secret gene encoded specifically for them to continue their legacy of greatness and unending competition.

Despite the vast amount of power with the perfect balance of poise and sensibility that I was lovingly staring up at, I was having a bit of a hard time making sense of what I had just seen. Jim Charge, my Number 1 to whom I trust implicitly and have pledged my unwavering allegiance to, just bit off the head of his pregnant mistress and ate it only to affix the re-animated head of the shoe department manager in its place seconds later. Not to mention that the monstrosity Jim Charge created in front of me proceeded to play with its tits for the first fifteen minutes of its existence. When the new pregnant Glenn-thing tried to lick its new nipples I finally spoke.

"This? This?" I sputtered while emphatically gesturing in the Glenn-thing's direction.

"This what, Number 2?"

Jim turned and his face caught the light just right highlighting how well-blended the blush that dusted his cheekbones was. Goddamn that man's beautiful aloofness.

"This is what . . . what . . . what you needed Glenn's head for?"

Jim Charge looked back and forth between the Glenn-thing and me with a puzzled look on his face.

"Of course it is. How else would I be able to keep my son's womb-body alive after I bit her head off? It's the same way I was born, and my father and the rest of the Charge men throughout history. What else would I use him for?"

I fought every urge to unleash a slew of questions and thinly veiled judgments, which would not only be an insult to my Number 1 but also something a good Number 2 would never do. I hid my unease with no problem, but the anger of still having to deal with Glenn burned hot deep inside of me.

"Actually," I said with the steady voice of a sober judge, "now that you mention it, that makes perfect sense. I don't know what else you would ever do with the severed head of a shoe department manager besides the scenario in which you just did."

"All right," said Jim Charge firmly. "Good then. Let's go."

"Yes sir," I said. "Where are we going?"

"Isn't it obvious? Look at this guy." Jim Charge pointed at the Glenn-thing. "I've got to redo his makeup and pronto. What the hell happened to you out there anyway? It looks like someone did a layup with your head, put you in a net and dropped on you on your face a bunch of times."

Jim Charge was far more perceptive than I initially thought as demonstrated through this brilliant deduction. It made me wonder if he was imbued with a power that allowed him to see through my eyes whenever he wanted to, simply because I was his Number 2. I didn't know if it was true, but I hoped it was. Anything that bonded me closer to the man who was my Number 1 was just fine by me.

"It's funny that you mention it," said the Glenn-thing. Jim put his hand on its shoulder to lead it back toward the area that had been the shrine.

"Can it ugly," said Jim, still smiling. "You're here to operate the body of my son's womb, not talk to me. Now head back to the storage closet and start re-stacking those boxes."

Glenn-thing opened its mouth to retort but struggled with silence instead. Glenn-thing hung its head, knowing there was nothing he could say even if he *could* think of what *to* say. Jim Charge was in charge, and Glenn-thing knew it.

"Good work, Number 2," said Jim Charge, turning to extend his hand to me. "Now come help me beautify this ugly bastard."

At that moment any doubts I had about my Number 1 were burned down and ripped out from the roots, never to sprout again. I stepped across three feet of broken glass and wet particleboard to give him my hand, which all but disappeared into its massiveness.

"Jim," I said as we walked behind Glenn-thing toward the back of the department.

"Yes Number 2?"

"I love you."

"I know Number 2, I know. I love you, too."

John Wayne Comunale

Chapter Eleven

Glenn-thing sat on a stack of empty lipstick crates in front of the shrine. Surprisingly it was intact despite the insane amount of destruction caused from Jim and Missy's battle and then from the fuck-fest that ensued shortly thereafter. Atop the shrine in the same place that Glenn's head had been now sat a chunk of glass from one of the many mirrors that used to populate the counter. Jim Charge stood directly behind the seated Glenn-thing studying its reflection intently to ensure the makeup he'd just applied was to his liking.

"Well," said Jim Charge, "it's not my best, but it'll have to do."

He was being modest and slightly self-deprecating because it was one of the best makeup jobs I had ever seen done in my entire life. If I hadn't been there myself to actually watch it take place I would never have thought that one person could have made Glenn-thing look so good, especially since I knew how absolutely hideous he really was. Jim Charge had somehow managed to soften and feminize Glenn's head so that it actually somewhat complimented the woman's body that it was now attached to. In fact it was such a job well done that you had to look long and hard to realize that it was a man's head that was staring back at you from atop this obviously pregnant female body.

"I think she looks . . . breathtaking," I finally managed.

"It's a complete one-eighty change for the better."

"Yeah, yeah," said Glenn-thing, taking a final look in the mirror before spinning around to face Jim Charge, "but what's the deal with this whole new pregnant body of mine? I mean, don't get me wrong, it's kind of cool but it's also kind of fucked up at the same time."

"This is how it has always been with all of the Charge men," said Jim. "Every one of us who has impregnated a woman with a new Charge man has bitten off the head of the mother and attached something else in its place to keep the body running until it's time."

"I hate to be the one to ask," said Glenn-thing, turning back around to the mirror for another peek, "but why in the absolute hell do you guys do that?"

"It's part of what feeds our competitive side, and is a crucial element in making us who we are," continued Jim. "The Charge men cannot be soft, and the origin of every person's softness comes from their relationship with their mother. Eliminate the mother, eliminate the softness."

"Why not wait for the kid to be born and then take him from his mother? What's with all the head eating during utero?"

"We have to remove the potential for weakness from the start. If a Charge man were left in a normal woman for its entire gestation period, there's potential for a bond to be made between mother and child while the baby is in the womb. By doing it this way we eliminate the chance of that happening."

Glenn-thing continued asking Jim Charge the same basic question of why in several different ways while I stood by waiting for my next order. It was quite clear that none of this made any sense to Glenn-thing, but it wasn't his job to understand any of it. His job was to basically keep the bun baking in the oven and nothing else. Jim Charge had made that quite clear earlier, and I could only hope that once the baby Charge was born I'd be rid of

Glenn in any form once and for all.

"Oh shit," said Glenn-thing. He grabbed the bump on his stomach that had gotten noticeably bigger since he'd sat down. "I think the baby is kicking or something. It feels like it has steel-toed boots on."

"Ah yes," said Jim Charge, placing his giant hand down on top of Glenn-thing's stomach to feel as well. "Those aren't steel-toes, though. They feel more like wingtips to me, which makes perfect sense at this stage in his development."

"This stage?" Glenn-thing looked mildly worried now, but I could tell he was trying to hide it from Jim Charge. "Are you telling me this kid actually has shoes on inside of me? How is that possible? How is this kid even this big anyway, I mean, didn't you *just* knock Missy up a few hours ago?"

"You're a severed head attached to a pregnant woman's body that you now have complete control over, and these are the questions you ask?"

Jim Charge took his hand from Glenn-thing's stomach and stepped back from the shrine. He plucked his tree trunk of a cigar from an ashtray he'd made out of a broken hollow mannequin head and puffed it back to life without the aid of a lighter.

"Gentlemen," started Jim as he began pacing back and forth in front of the shrine, "in case you haven't realized it yet, time is of the essence. Charge men have a gestation period that can be as short as two days but no longer than a week. My grandfather still boasts of how he burst from his carrier-womb after thirty minutes because his dick had already gotten so big there wasn't enough room for the two of them. He's since grown into his dick, and while that story can't be proved it can't be disproved either. "

Glenn-thing shot a worried glance my way as he rubbed his stomach again. I imagined he was wondering if at any moment a giant dick was going to rip through his stomach and release the Charge boy inside of him, who would then turn around and beat him to death with the large, engorged member. The thought made me chuckle as I hoped against hope for something like that to happen.

"My point is this, fellow," said Jim. He released a monstrously large puff of smoke that danced around the shrine, giving the thing a whole new and somewhat mystic appearance. "We haven't much time. If I'm going to fulfill my destiny and follow the path of my lineage, I need to act fast, and by I, I mean we."

"Yes sir," I said, eager to please my Number 1. "I'll do whatever it takes to make it happen. I hope you know that, sir."

"Of course I do, Number 2, and I truly appreciate it. I think it's safe to say after that last minor tussle and the current shape of the department store's final line of management that we can definitively say that we have conquered the store. At least there's no one left to contest that statement. Now it's time to move on to the next conquest."

"You mean you're gonna' take over the rest of the mall?" asked Glenn-thing.

"The mall, my short-sighted friend," said Jim, "the mall is small potatoes, and by all intents and purposes is already ours. No my friends, we are going to take over these United States of America in the name of Charge Land, thereby shoving it down my father and grandfather's throats as well as my unborn son's. Then there will be no doubt who the dominant Charge man is and always will be."

Chapter Twelve

"That's right you old bastard," said Jim Charge into the phone that I had dug out of the rubble behind the makeup counter. It was pretty busted up, but Jim Charge somehow got it to work, not that I ever doubted he could. "Well, I will say it to your face if you bring your wrinkled-up, cowardly, no balls-havin' ass down here to Charge Land! Oh yeah? I'd like to see you try that. Fine then. Yes, this means war. I'll see you soon, then. Goodbye."

Jim Charge dropped the receiver to the ground where it smacked hard against the tile and broke into even more pieces than before.

"Who was that?" I asked, eager to see who my Number 1 was ripping into.

"That was the president. I've officially declared war on the United States in the name of Charge Land."

"What? No shit?" I was excited and panicked at the same time. "What should we do? Where should we go? What's our battle plan? Where are our weapons? What do we . . ."

"Number 2," said Jim Charge, "with all due respect please shut the hell up. This isn't the kind of conventional war like you're thinking. The president is on his way here for what will no doubt be a drawn out and overblown pissing contest."

"Pissing contest?"

"Yes, a pissing contest. That's how almost every major world issue gets solved. The rest of it, the guns, tanks, bombs, that's all for show. Merely pomp and circumstance."

"You mean like that song?" chimed in Glenn-thing from where it sat inclined on a pile of moist cardboard and mannequin arms. Glenn-thing's stomach had swelled even more in the last hour.

"What did I tell you earlier about talking?" Jim shot a look that could have sliced Glenn's head clean off for the second time, and he promptly slumped down to avoid the sharp sightline.

"Okay," I said. "Pissing contest, huh? I can get behind that. So how do we prepare for this *pissing contest*?"

"*We* don't prepare anything. This is something I have to do on my own. *Mano a mano*."

"But . . . but . . ." I stammered, crestfallen at the thought of my Number 1 not needing me. "Surely I can do something to help you prepare?"

"You could make your way out to the food court and get me a burger and some ice cream," said Glenn-thing. "I got used to not being hungry after I didn't have a body and all, but now that I'm pregnant I am starving."

"Can it, jerk-wad," I spat in Glenn-thing's direction. "No one cares what you need."

"But I'm so hungry," Glenn-thing whined. "Please . . . think of the baby."

"You don't need to eat," said Jim Charge to the monstrosity that was carrying his son. "The child will drain your new body of all the nutrients it needs until it's ready to be born. Besides, we don't have time for foolishness anyway. The president will be here soon, and I'll need the two of you here with me."

Hearing Jim Charge say that he *needed* me here with him sent warm waves of pleasure up my spine not unlike those caused by orgasm. I ignored the fact that he included Glenn-thing in the comment since he clearly didn't *need* him in the same way he needed me. He just needed to keep Glenn-thing close in order to monitor how fast the pregnancy was moving along. It made perfect sense since he needed to complete his conquest before his son was born in order to ensure he'd out-done him before he even entered the world, or at least that's what I told myself. I snapped from my daydream and saw Jim Charge had directed his attention to the ceiling, studying it intently.

"What is it sir?" I asked. "Is it the president? Is he here?"

"No, but he's close."

Jim Charge suddenly jumped straight up in the air and punched his arm through the ceiling that was twelve feet above us. He caught hold of something beneath the flimsy tiles and yanked down with all of his weight. A moment later he was falling back to the ground where he landed safely on his feet bringing down with him a broken pipe that supplied the sprinkler system with water. The long length of pipe started in his hand, and disappeared back up into the ceiling through the hole he had punched.

The end of the pipe gushed a strong stream of water from its jagged, exposed broken end, which happened to be pointed directly at Glenn-thing. The water hit him with the intensity of a fire hose and knocked him from his reclining position to the floor, and I laughed to myself suppressing a full on giggle fit.

"Whoops! Sorry about that Glenn," said Jim Charge, who clearly didn't mean for it to happen. "Boy, am I glad we used waterproof mascara on you this time."

Jim Charge stuck the broken pipe that was spilling out gallons of water by the second right into his mouth. He stood there swallowing down the water just as fast as it was coming out. He even pulled it away for a second to replace it with his cigar from which he took three enormous puffs before switching it back out for the pipe.

He drank the tremendous quantity of water like it was something he did on a regular basis, and from seeing this I had to believe he did. Despite the many gallons that were clearly streaming into his body, he showed no signs of swelling in the least. I had no idea where he was putting it all. Just then I heard a humming sound that I thought was just in my head until it became increasingly louder. Jim heard it too and looked back up at the ceiling, the pipe still dangling from his mouth. The sound was loud and right on top of us now. Jim Charge pulled the steel pipe from his mouth and squeezed the opening shut with one hand as if he were kinking a hose.

"He's here," said Jim with a smile. "The president is here. It's almost go time."

With that Jim Charge shed his current suit for a black on black tuxedo complete with tails and a top hat that sprouted out from his head. The rumbling, which I deduced was the product of military helicopters hovering above the department store, began to slow and then stopped all together. Jim's eyes stayed glued to the ceiling and followed a loud banging of falling footsteps. The pounding came again, louder and harder, and then one more time before chunks of the ceiling crashed down in front of me, and I stepped back to keep from being flattened.

The dust settled a second later and there, standing directly between my Number 1 and me, was the president. His frame was long and caricature-thin save for the bowling ball size lump of a beer gut held tightly in place by a white dress shirt one size too small. His suit was gray, but not that particularly nice considering he was the leader of the free world. His tie was an uninspired dull red color, and even the American flag pin attached to his suit jacket, perched just above his heart where you'd expect it to be, seemed faded and lusterless. His face was wrinkled up into a Dirty Harry-esque snarl, his left eye squinting hate-rays in the direction of my

Number 1. One thing was for sure, the president was one ugly son of a bitch.

Jim Charge, whose custom tuxedo and devilish good looks made the president look even worse by comparison, smiled and put his hands at his side like he was about to draw a pair of invisible pistols from make-believe holsters.

"Hello Mr. President," he said. "Welcome to Ch—"

That was all that Jim had the time to get out because in the brief two seconds it took him to say those words the president had yanked down his zipper, whipped out his thin veiny dick and shot from it a high pressured bright yellow piss stream directly at Jim Charge's head, or at least where his head had been. All of a sudden Jim was just gone and the long, arching stream of piss passed right through the space he had just occupied. The errant piss-rocket hit Glenn-thing in the face.

"Aughhgrrrglll," said Glenn-thing as the piss went into his open mouth and smacked against his duodenum. "Ahh, come on man. That's piss for Christ's sake!"

The president cut off his stream with no problem, clutched his less than stellar cock hard and scanned the area around him for signs of Jim Charge while cursing under his breath. Just then Jim floated slowly and silently down not four feet behind the president, holding what looked like the fat end of a Louisville slugger out in front of him. It wasn't until Jim landed and grabbed the bat with both hands that I realized it was actually his tremendously thick cock. Piss erupted from the freakish thing like water from an open hydrant and struck the president right in the back of the head.

The force propelled him across the makeup department and right into Glenn-thing who was wiping his face with a towel. He dropped it from his eyes just in time to see the presidential-pecker slap him across the face followed closely by the piss stream that propelled the president there. The president and Glenn-thing hit the floor in a tangled heap while still being showered in Jim Charge's piss. The stream cut off as quickly as it had shot out, and the president wasted no time in getting to his feet. His snarl was unwavering as he wiped piss from his face on the back of his arm and shot through the air toward Jim Charge like he had a jet engine shoved up his ass.

I watched the president close the gap between the two of them in a matter of seconds. He held his dick with both hands to keep it from flapping in the wind and took aim at Jim Charge's face. The president was fast, but Jim was faster, and he bent backwards at the knees making his body run horizontally against the ground. That caused Jim's sizable salami to stick straight up in the air where it just so happened to meet the president's face, effectively counteracting his momentum. Jim Charge delivered such a mighty dick-slap to the president that it sent him hurdling like a ragdoll back in the direction he'd come from.

"Jesus jam a poker in my ass, and call me daddy Christ!" yelled Glenn-thing, finally managing to get his balance in the puddle of piss and stand up. "What in the hell is with all the pi—?"

That was all Glenn-thing got out before the freshly cock-smacked president slammed back into him, dick first again, and sent them both back down into the piss puddle.

"It's called a pissing match," said Jim Charge. "It's how almost every world conflict is settled. Didn't you hear me earlier?"

"Almost all?" I asked. "How do they solve the rest of the conflicts?"

"Cock showing contest," said Jim Charge, now standing straight up and shedding his tuxedo.

In its place appeared a canary colored, double-breasted, Admiral-style suit made entirely out of rain slickers. Then he jumped through the air toward the president, who was still tangled up with Glenn-thing in the piss. Jim Charge landed in front of them just as the president made it to his feet and pulled Glenn-thing up with him. He held Glenn-thing to his side tight with his left hand and in his right was a giant Bowie knife held up against the swollen belly of the hybrid creature.

"Take another step, and I'll cut your son right out of this monster's belly and drown him with my piss," growled the president. A purple cock-shaped bruise was already forming down the middle of his face.

"Okay, okay," said Jim, taking his hands off of his dick and holding them up in front of him. "We can work this out without resorting to—"

"Don't tell me what we can do, son," interrupted the president. "You see, you are in no position to tell me anything. I'm holding all the cards. You understand? The only thing we're gonna' do is exactly what I say, or I will relieve your unborn child and this hideous thing of their lives."

I shot a nervous look up to my Number 1's face, but found no sign that he shared the sentiment. His facial expression reflected only the cool calmness that I had no reason to not expect from my Number 1. What I thought was at first a trick of the light turned out to be Jim Charge smiling.

"That kind of tickles," said Glenn-thing, gesturing down toward the knife pressed hard against the fast growing, baby-filled belly.

"Shut up," said the president and Jim Charge in unison.

"Now, you listen to me," said the president, continuing his exchange with Jim Charge. "You started this thing, but I aim on ending it. And while, yes, we will work this out, I think a bit of violence will have to be resorted to."

The president ground his perfectly white, old-man teeth together and spit the grit in the face of Glenn-thing. The presidential throat oyster dangled from the tip of Glenn-thing's nose, defying gravity's need to pull it down to the ground. I looked at Jim for a reaction, but all he did was smile wider, and I dropped my eyes to the floor to keep myself from laughing. That was when I saw what Jim Charge was smiling for.

He had let go of his mammoth cock at the president's request, this much was true, but now the head of Jim's dick had snaked its way into the newly re-opened pipe he had been sucking water from earlier. I didn't see it happen, but I assume it was the tip of Jim's dick that had pried the pipe back open and inserted itself inside without the help of his hands, which were clearly still being held in the air. My eyes traced the pipe from between Jim's legs, along the floor close to twenty feet back to where it shot back up into the ceiling. Through the torn and broken ceiling tiles I followed the pipe back in Jim's direction running past him to the sprinkler head that was positioned directly above the president.

"What in the glorious hell do you think is so funny?" snarled the President as he too noticed the smile growing across Jim's face.

Just then a few tiny droplets of piss dripped down from the sprinkler head onto the president's nose. A second later a few more drops hit his cheek, then more fell across his thin, twisted lips.

"What in the he—"

That was all the president got out before the sprinkler head exploded off, and from it flowed gallons and gallons of Jim Charge's highly pressurized piss. The super piss blast knocked Glenn-thing and the president to the floor and sent them flying off in different directions. The large knife the president held shot across the floor and skidded to a stop at my feet. I picked it up gingerly and shook as much piss from it as possible before holding the grip tight in my hand. I figured I should be ready to protect my Number 1 if the president was somehow able to counterstrike.

The piss rocketed out of the broken sprinkler head with no sign of letting up, and I looked over at Jim whose dick was still jammed into the pipe. His hands were on his hips, and he was laughing loud enough to be heard over the waterfall-like piss-gusher that he was powering with urine created from water he drank from that very same pipe not ten minutes ago. I turned back toward where Glenn-thing and the president had stood before being washed away by piss that was now almost two inches deep throughout the entire area of the once pristine makeup counter.

I struck a battle pose, bending my knees with the knife held out in front of me, and stared in the direction of where he had just been standing, acting as if I knew exactly where he had gone. Suddenly through the falling piss stream I saw a silhouette approaching, and I adjusted my battle pose to allow for optimal killing. As the water parted I relaxed when I saw it was a very dazed Glenn-thing, soaking wet, looking extremely confused. He shambled forward through the piss-falls, took a few steps toward Jim with has arms out in front of him, and then promptly dropped to his knees and fell over face first. The splash he created sent piss-droplets right into my open mouth, and I spat while cursing Glenn-thing who lay there unconscious. His face was down in the quickly rising piss lake, and the bare ass of his newly acquired pregnant female body was pointed up in the air due to the negligee it wore being bunched up under the swollen, child-filled belly.

Before either of us could even think about helping Glenn-thing up, not that I particularly wanted to, there came a shrill whoop from the far side of the falling water-wall of piss. I looked up to see the president jump through the translucent stream holding in his outstretched arm a wire hanger, the hook end on perfect course to meet Glenn-thing's exposed and vulnerable snatch. The president knew there was more than one way to skin a cat, and he was determined to stop the Charge lineage from continuing.

Jim Charge shot through the air in a flash from where he stood. His long and mighty cock flapped across his hip and waved in the air behind him like the tail of a tiger jumping down onto an unsuspecting gazelle. He met the president in mid-air just before the tip of the hanger reached the moist and slightly dilated vagina of Glenn-thing. Jim clamped his massive hand on the president's wrist and twisted, crushing the old cowboy's bones while keeping the hangar from finding its mark. At the same time with his other hand Jim grabbed hold of the president's soda straw of a cock and yanked.

I heard a pop followed by what sounded like the snap of an elastic waistband as the two men's bodies collided with each other and fell backward with Jim on top of the president. A huge wave of piss exploded upward and out, drenching everything within a fifty-foot radius of where the two landed. I, being unfortunately located in the splash zone, was not spared from the complete and thorough piss soaking that the four of us now shared in.

"Oh god," I said, I spat the acrid tanginess of the two men's piss out while searching desperately for a dry garment to wipe my eyes with, but of course there was nothing. After this I doubted highly that there would be any item left in the entire store that wasn't tainted with piss.

I blinked the ammonia out of eyes enough to see Jim Charge still lying on top of the president directly beneath the piss stream that had now dwindled to a slow trickle since my Number 1 was no longer pumping urine through it. Neither of the men moved, and Glenn-thing was still unconscious lying face down, ass up a few feet away. He could've been dead for all I knew. In that moment my stomach sank as the thought that I might possibly be completely alone whipped itself through my head along with a myriad of terrifying consequences that could be in store for me.

"Jim?" I called, stepping forward timidly. "Sir? Sir, are

you okay? Do you need help?"

Just then the two of them erupted into a coughing fit, both trying to rid their lungs of the excess urine that had accumulated within them. The president sputtered and spat thick and bloody loogies off to the side while trying to lift the tank-like frame of Jim Charge off of him. Jim's back expanded to nearly twice its normal size as he breathed deep and coughed a sickening mixture of piss, phlegm, bile and any number of slimy horrors that lived inside of him directly down into the president's face. Jim Charge pushed himself up and stood, looming large over the small and crumpled president, who was now violently vomiting. Dangling from Jim's right hand I saw the pathetic presidential penis. It was ghost-white and left much to be desired in the girth department. Jim held it up, smiled and wiggled the thing down at the president. I thought it very much resembled a raw hotdog, which actually reminded me of how hungry I was getting.

"Jim Charge, you son of a bitch!" yelled the president up at him between heaves. "You give that back to me this instant."

"I could," replied Jim, "but that's no fun."

Jim opened his mouth, popped the president's dick in and swallowed it down like it was nothing. I have to admit that while I did not see that coming it still seemed like the perfect thing to do in this exact moment.

"What! Nooooooo," shrieked the president. "Why?!?"

"Sorry Mr. President," said Jim Charge. "Nothing personal, you understand, but necessary. I assume you'll be conceding the country over to me now?"

Just then a huge hole in the ceiling ripped open above where the president lay and flooded Charge Land with a loud rush of sound and wind. A rope ladder fell down through the hole from the big black helicopter hovering above the store and hit the now dick-less president in the chest.

"You may have won this one," said the president,

grabbing the bottom rung of the ladder, "but I'll be back!"

"Well," said Jim, belching, "I did just rip your dick off and ate it, so I think that means I pretty much won them all."

The president clutched the last rung of the rope ladder and the helicopter began lifting him into the air and out of the department store. Just before he disappeared through the hole in the ceiling, the president pointed down at Jim Charge and sneered the most sneering sneer that has probably ever been sneered in all of presidential history.

"This isn't over, Charge," he yelled down to us below.

"Actually it is," Jim called back. "Remember what I just said about ripping your dick off? That's the definition of 'over,' if you ask me. See you in hell."

The president vanished through the ceiling as the helicopter whisked him off with Jim Charge below giving a tongue-in-cheek mock salute to the mangled man while I just gave him the finger. A moment later the chopper was gone, and we were left in dark, piss-soaked silence once again. The silence was broken a moment later by the sputtering coughs of Glenn-thing as he came to and rolled over onto his back.

"What . . . what happened?" Glenn-thing finally managed after coughing up a majority of the piss he had inadvertently consumed in the melee. Glenn-thing blinked a few times and looked around before answering his own question. "Oh yeah. Did we win?"

"I think so," I said. I turned to Jim who was still looking up at the hole the president had just escaped through. "We did, right?"

The yellow, rain slicker suit Jim was wearing burst apart at the seams and fell to floor around him as a new suit materialized in its place. The suit was dark brown, made of wool and had leather patches on the elbows like something a college professor would wear. The pale yellow dress shirt that sprouted across his pec-dominated chest was accented nicely by a wide tie decorated with a paisley pattern spotted with accent colors akin to the shirt and suit. The rain boots on his feet melted down nicely to form a pair of freshly shined penny loafers complete with one new penny apiece. The cuffs on his slacks stopped about three inches short of the top of his shoes creating the perfect high-water pants that were actually quite functional given that we were still standing in several inches of piss.

It was truly one of the most hideous suits I had ever seen from a by-gone era that was trying hard itself to forget the fashion *faux pas* committed during its reign in time. As much as I wanted to hate this new suit for all of the obvious reasons, I just couldn't. Jim Charge once again pulled off the long outdated look with the ease and unwavering confidence of someone who had just won control of a country after ripping off the former leader's penis and eating it. I didn't know much, but I did know that when it came to fashion Jim Charge was infallible.

"We won all right, Number 2," said Jim, turning towards me, smiling, "but I have a feeling the former leader of the free world does not see it as being so."

"Is he coming back?" asked Glenn-thing. He sat up and tried to roll his awkward, pregnant body over to try and stand.

"I'd be a fool to think that he wasn't, even though he clearly lost the pissing match, but sometimes you gotta' take a second run at these hardheaded, prideful leader-types."

"So what do we do now?" I asked, still holding the handle of the large knife with a white-knuckle death grip.

"We wait, Number 2," said Jim, reaching down to help Glenn-thing up. "We wait."

John Wayne Comunale

Chapter Thirteen

I found a push broom in the pile of junk Jim had discarded from the storage closet when he erected his shrine and used it to push as much of the standing piss that I could away from the hardly recognizable makeup counter. I did my best to use the broken pieces of fixtures and piles of ruined clothing to create a path that would send the piss I was pushing down the aisle, towards the store's entrance, and through the barred gates. I worked on this while Jim Charge attended to once again fix the makeup of Glenn-thing that had been completely ruined from all the piss. Jim didn't have to fix his own makeup, though, since it just appeared on him much like his suits did. His current face displayed a more subdued natural look overall with the exception of the dramatically thick, Cleopatra-style eyeliner that grew out from around his lids.

I pushed as much of the piss that I could away from our Charge Land home base but getting rid of all of it would be close to impossible without some industrial strength equipment. I imagined the piss would just dry over time leaving our illustrious new kingdom coated in a sticky yellow crust that smelled of the expelled kidney-filtered waste of two world titans. Or at least one titan and one skinny, washed up, limp-dick, wannabe loser, but either way I'm sure that after a while we'd all get used to the smell. It would become a part of us.

I took another look out over the ravaged and unrecognizable wasteland that had not so long ago been a department store. While I will forever hold this place in high regard being the birthplace of Charge Land, it was clear we were going to have to find someplace else to headquarter out of. If we had indeed won, as Jim assured me we had, then we should have quite a few options to choose from. I'd love to move to the Rocky Mountains and build a monster log cabin mansion to fly the Charge Land flag out in front of, but it didn't matter what I wanted. Jim Charge was firmly in charge and as his Number 2 I was bound to support his decisions even if it meant staying in a half-burned down, piss soaked department store.

I chucked my broom into a pile of broken floor display fixtures and mannequin bits and headed back toward the storage room where Jim and Glenn-thing were. Jim was putting the finishing touches on Glenn-thing's makeup and using the mirror from atop the shrine to inspect his work. Glenn-thing sat on a stack of wilted Revlon nail polish boxes made flimsy from the amount of urine that had soaked into them. The boxes rocked as Glenn-thing grabbed at his stomach with both hands clearly in pain.

"It won't be much longer," said Jim Charge, holding Glenn-thing's grimacing head in place with one hand while applying lip liner with the other. "Now quit squirming and stop moving your mouth."

"So," I said casually, stepping between Glenn-thing and the shrine, "what's our next move, sir? Should I prepare for us to head to Washington and take over the White House? Do you think they're expecting us?"

"Whether or not they're expecting us is not the issue," said Jim, working bright pink rouge into Glenn-thing's cheeks. "It's getting that no-dick-having, washed-up cowboy of a president to realize that he's lost, is the issue."

Just then there came a clatter from above in the

direction of the hole in the ceiling that the president had escaped through. The sound pushed my heart up into my throat, and I reached to my side for the Bowie knife, forgetting that I'd left it back by the broom. Jim Charge was clearly unaffected by the noise and continued making up Glenn-thing, not allowing his attention to be diverted from his present task. I looked from Jim to the hole and saw a small black box with a flashing red light attached to a tiny parachute falling slowly to the ground.

"Uh, sir," I said, pointing to where the box landed.

"Right on time," said Jim, still not looking up from Glenn-thing's face. "Be a lamb, Number 2, and go grab that box for me."

I almost asked Jim Charge how he knew what it was but thought better of it. A good Number 2 never questions his Number 1, after all. I rushed over to the box, maneuvering around the broken fixtures and stomping through puddles of piss. When I reached the box I saw that it had a screen on the front that made it look like a miniature television. I snatched it up and rushed back to Jim, curious myself to see what this odd delivery could be.

When I reached the shrine Jim was finished with Glenn-thing's makeup and was standing back admiring his work once again. He had shed suits in the short time it took me to get the box and now wore a classic looking black suit with a white shirt; a black skinny tie dangled from his neck and three-inch creepers sprouted from his feet to complete the new-wave look. I placed the tiny TV in the outstretched hand of Jim Charge and positioned myself behind him so I could watch. He seemed to know exactly what it was and pushed a button on the side that I didn't notice was there the entire time I carried it. The screen on the box lit up with static and snow for only a moment before we were staring at the face of the president. The bruise Jim's cock had left on his face was a rich and dark purple, and the swelling had increased a significant amount since he'd left Charge Land.

"Hello again, assholes," said the president from the screen. "I told you this wasn't over."

"I recall you saying something along those lines," said Jim to the screen. "Oh hey, how's your dick doing again? Oh wait, that's right."

"Very funny Charge, but I have at this very moment the top dick scientists in the country working non-stop on a new dick for me that will make your pathetic wang look like string bean casserole by comparison."

"I'm not even sure that makes sense," replied Jim. "I've had some pretty excellent string bean casseroles in my life that could make a genetically grown dick look pretty bad."

"Shut up, prick," snapped the president, "you know what I mean. Anyway, it's not going to matter soon because I'm about to turn your dick *and* the rest of you into string bean casserole. Take a look at this."

The screen cut from the close up of the president to a wide shot of a lush green field. A hole in the middle of the field opened up and from it rose a large nuclear missile. Smoke and fire shot from the bottom of the missile and a second later it rocketed off into the air and out of frame. The screen cut back to the president who was cackling maniacally.

"Hey there, Jim," he said. "Guess where that little puppy is heading. See you in hell. Maybe you can convince the devil to let you take over the lake of fire. Toot-a-loo, jerk off!"

The screen went black and Jim Charge crushed the box in his hand like it was made out of tissue paper, but I wasn't worried. Sure, a nuclear missile being launched right at us seemed like a pretty major deal, but Jim Charge had proved over and over to me that he had everything under control and always would. That's why he was Jim Charge.

"Huh," said Jim, frowning and looking at the floor. "I

have to say, I wasn't expecting that."
　Shit.

John Wayne Comunale

Chapter Fourteen

I clung firmly to the thin steel cylinder rungs of the ladder on the side of the water tower that stood watch over the mall parking lot. I was more than three-quarters of the way up but had been frozen at this spot for the last ten or so minutes. I knew I shouldn't have looked down, but now I was staring in disbelief at the vast amount of space between the ground and myself. I gasped and nearly dropped the bobby pin from my mouth, which was the only reason I was climbing up there to begin with. After Jim watched the message the president sent him, he thought for a few minutes while pacing back and forth between puddles of piss.

His suit shed and changed every time he turned on his heels to pace in the opposite direction. He went from new-wave black, to nerd-linger powdered blue with a ruffle shirt, to a pink and mauve leisure suit, to a fringe-laden, brown western-style suit complete with bolo tie and finally to a deep blue zoot suit with fine silver pinstripes running throughout. Jim Charge stopped and snatched the watch from his pocket that was attached to his pants by a comically long chain.

"We have just enough time," he said, snapping the watch closed and shoving it back into his pocket.

"Time for what?" I asked, eager to hear his master plan.

"No time to tell you now," he said. "Number 2, go find

a bobby pin and meet me at the top of the water tower in the parking lot. Glenn-thing, you stay here and don't get killed until you have a chance to push my son out, but don't push him out until I get back."

"A bobby pin? What do you need a . . ."

That was all I could say before Jim Charge disappeared. I looked over at Glenn-thing who seemed more than happy to do nothing as he kicked off his heels and reclined in the makeup chair. I stood frozen for a moment, unsure of what to do exactly, but then Glenn-thing farted loudly, and I suddenly found the motivation to get moving. Next thing I know I'm climbing the water tower, fear-stricken and frozen in place. Where the hell was Jim Charge? I'd only really looked down because I was sure he'd be following me up the ladder by now, but he wasn't. I didn't see him anywhere, and although I know a good Number 2 never questions his Number 1, it was very hard for me not scream *why the hell am I doing this* from the side of that tower.

I choked back my fear and banished it from my mind. After all, Jim Charge may possibly have the ability to read my thoughts. I bit down hard on the bobby pin and ground the soft metal between my teeth as I convinced myself it was okay to loosen my death grip on the ladder rung and continue my ascent. By this point I knew better than to question Jim Charge, and if he wanted me to sit at the top of a water tower with a bobby pin between my teeth, then so be it. I watched this man rip the dick off of the president of the United States of America, and based on that alone I don't think there's much life can throw at Jim Charge that he can't rip the dick off of, including a nuclear missile.

I reached the final rung of the ladder and pulled myself up onto the curved metal top of the tower. I was so surprised to see that I wasn't alone, I gasped, and the bobby pin shot to the back of my throat where it became lodged in my duodenum. My hands went to my throat, and I stepped back off the ladder and onto thin air. In that terrifying moment the only thing I could think was that I hoped I choked to death before I hit the ground so I wouldn't have to feel my body burst like a ripe melon when I hit the pavement. Suddenly I wasn't falling backwards anymore and was in fact falling upward. That was when I realized that Jim Charge had a firm grasp on my right forearm and was pulling me back to safety. That is if you can call the top of the water tower "safety."

My mouth was agape as I gasped for air, and Jim shoved the hand he wasn't holding me with into my mouth and pulled out the bobby pin. He put me down, and I coughed and hacked for several minutes as I attempted to speak. How in hell did he beat me to the top? The only access to the top was the ladder that I climbed, and I knew he didn't use that way. Still, there he was sitting cross-legged with several boxes of cosmetic products set to either side of him. The suit he wore now was an exact three-piece replica of the outfit daredevil Evel Knievel used to wear, complete with red, white and blue sequins. His makeup had changed to a subdued even-coated base with his eyes lined in dramatically thick black eyeliner. The makeup around his eyes made him look downright scary. I finally regained the ability to speak and shouted in frustration.

"How the hell did you get up here? I didn't see you on the ladder, and I know you didn't get to it before me, and why the hell didn't you bring a bobby pin yourself if you brought all this other stuff!"

"Come on now, Number 2," said Jim Charge in a soft tone quite contradictory to my own. "You know better than to question your Number 1."

I did. I did know that, and my heart sank to hear him have to say it out loud to me. It was only a few minutes ago that I was praising my Number 1's ability to fly fearless in the face of danger and rip its dick off, and here I am now with doubts and questions in the same breath. I honestly wouldn't blame Jim Charge if he grabbed me by my pencil neck and tossed me right off the water tower. Jim loomed over me, looking down on my pathetic, doubt-filled, sad-sack, excuse for a body and raised his arms. I closed my eyes and prepared to accept whatever fate my Number 1 was about to bestow upon me, fully aware that I was not only about to lose my Number 1 but my life as well, and I deserved to lose both.

Jim Charge's powerful arms collapsed around me, squeezed tight and lifted me up off the ground. I held my eyes closed waiting for the feeling of falling to overtake me when Jim dropped me off the side. I felt the massive head of my Number 1 pressed up against the side of my neck between my head and shoulder, and I opened my eyes. To my surprise Jim Charge wasn't holding me over the edge waiting for just the right moment to toss me down to my much deserved death. He was hugging me. He was hugging me extremely tight while swaying ever so gently back and forth. I was shocked to the point that I didn't even realize I had brought my arms up and wrapped them around Jim in reciprocation of his gesture.

Just as the pressure of the embrace upon my skeletal structure was about to reach the point of crushing my bones into dust, Jim subsided and held me out in front of him so that I was looking directly into his eyes. A single tear rolled down the more than perfect bone structure of Jim's face without marring his eye makeup in the least. As I stared into his watery eyes I felt a rush of emotions overcome me, and in that moment there was so much I wanted to say to Jim Charge. I wanted to tell him that I loved him. I wanted to tell him how in our short time together he'd become the most important person in my life. I wanted to tell him that he'd saved me. I wanted to tell him thank you. That was when the whistling started, and both of our heads snapped up to track the sound's origin.

Jim set me down, turned around and pointed up in the

sky at something heading straight for us and fast. I didn't have to even look to know it was the missile the president had fired at us. Jim wasted no time gathering the boxes of beauty supplies up. He was able to hold them all under each of his overly muscled arms with no problem. The bobby pin I had been charged with bringing rested firmly in Jim's mouth between his perfect and polished chompers, the same way I had held it on my way up the tower.

"Don't worry, Number 2," said Jim, "this won't take long. Make sure that mutant inside doesn't push my son out until I get back."

Jim Charge turned his back to me, bent his knees slightly and leapt straight up into the air. I knew Jim Charge was special from the moment I met him, but I didn't realize he could defy the laws of gravity. He kept going up higher and higher until he was just another indistinguishable dot on the horizon. I watched the dot that was Jim Charge as it flew directly into the path of the missile and disappeared. The missile's trajectory did not change in the least as it barreled its way toward the department store. I frantically searched the sky in vain for any sign of Jim Charge, but when I turned my attention back to the missile I breathed a sigh of relief.

Jim was straddled atop the missile like he was trying to break a nuclear powered wild horse. I could tell that he'd ripped a panel from the thing and was elbow deep in its inner workings. Still, the missile's path was not changing, and in fact appeared to be picking up speed. I stood frozen, fully aware that there was nothing I could do to help my Number 1 now, and it terrified me. The missile screamed over the water tower a mere twenty feet from my head, and the force of rushing air knocked me backward and sent me skidding across the smooth steel of the water tower. Instinct and reflex took over as I slid off the edge, and my hand shot up and grabbed the top rung of the ladder I had used to get there.

I pulled myself close to the ladder and held tight with both hands as I watched the missile Jim was riding head right for the department store. This couldn't be the end. Not for Jim Charge and I. He'd taught me so much in our short time together that the thought of that being taken away all of sudden made me want to let go of the ladder and fall into oblivion. Just as the missile was about to strike the building a thought occurred to me, and all worry melted away. Jim Charge was *in charge*, and he always was. If Charge Land being destroyed by a missile fired from a dick-less president was not what he wanted to happen, then I truly believed that he wouldn't let it.

Sure enough, right before the tip of the missile struck the side of the department store Jim pulled hard on its guts, and it made ninety degree turn shooting straight back up into the sky. I clung to the side of the water tower and watched it climb higher and higher until it turned and started heading back in the direction it came from with Jim Charge still on top ripping away at the delicate technology inside. I watched the missile until it was too far way for me to even see the massive flame that propelled it glowing against darkened sky as dusk set in.

Chapter Fifteen

I remember someone telling me when I first started at the department store that there used to be a television in the break room, but that bitch Missy had locked it up in one of the cabinets because she said it encouraged employees to take more and longer breaks. I'd never seen this television, but as I ransacked the break room I prayed it was really there. After I'd lost sight of Jim Charge flying off on the back of the nuclear missile I knew I had to get to a television and see where he was going. Even if he crashed it into the ocean or rode it into the sun a la *Superman IV*, I figured that a man straddling a giant missile like a wild steer was enough to at least make the local news at five.

Once I had managed to work my way down the side of the water tower to the safety of the ground I rushed into Charge Land to first check on Glenn-thing to make sure he held the Charge-ling in his mutant womb, and to then find the phantom break room television. I burst into the backdoor of the department store and splashed through piss puddles and soggy ceiling tiles on my way to the makeup counter. Glenn-thing was still in the chair we'd left him in, but now he'd propped his feet up on Jim's shrine. He was moaning and holding his swollen stomach.

I rushed over and stuck my head between his legs to make sure Jim's son-to-be was safely inside. He was still in there for now, but I wasn't sure how long Glenn-thing would be able to hold him in. I stared into that swollen, pulsating vagina as it gargled and burped out thick yellow mucus strands that slowly dripped from the gaping thing. I pulled my head out from under the negligée and got up in Glenn-thing's face.

"You have to hold on," I said loudly. "Do you hear me? You have to keep that baby inside of you until Jim gets back."

"Ughhhhhh," moaned Glenn-thing. "It hurts so bad. I don't know how much longer I can . . ."

I interrupted Glenn-thing with a slap in the face, and then gave him another one just for good measure.

"You do know how much longer," I said, getting my face so close to his that our noses touched. "You *will* hold that baby inside of you for as long as it takes for Jim Charge to get back."

"When? When is he coming?" Glenn-thing screamed out with tears streaming down his bloated face, once again ruining his makeup.

"I'll be right back, and then I'll be able to tell you. Until then, you keep that pussy squeezed shut so tight the good lord himself couldn't get a pinky in there."

I turned and sprinted in the direction of the break room hoping that Missy Cummings had practiced doing kegel exercises with regularity before Glenn's head was fused to her body. I ripped apart every cabinet looking for the television and found nothing but stale remnants of forgotten salty snacks and several well-hidden travel-size whiskey bottles placed there by employees who needed a little something extra to get through the day.

The only place I hadn't looked was the small closet at the back of the room next to the microwave. I had never seen anyone go into the closet before to get anything and had always assumed that it was empty. I grabbed the knob and turned, but of course it was locked. I looked around and spotted the fire extinguisher bolted to the wall in the far left corner. I ripped it from the mounting and bashed at the knob of the closet until it broke off completely, and the door popped open. I chucked the extinguisher behind me and pulled the door open the rest of the way. The closet was completely empty except for a single twelve-inch screen black and white television with an antenna attached that looked more like it belonged in the backyard of a Ham radio enthusiast.

"What the hell?" I said out loud to myself. "This is the television that was distracting everyone? I'd rather watch the inside of Glenn-thing's asshole than try to watch this piece of shit."

I snatched it up, wiped a thick layer of dust off the screen and took off with it back to the makeup counter hoping that it still worked. When I got there Glenn-thing was moaning and clutching his stomach, but now there was an obvious amount of motion going on inside the womb. I could see tiny hands and feet pushing out from the inside of Glenn-thing, trying to break through the fleshy membrane to escape. A wave of flesh undulated back and forth across Glenn-thing's stomach like the magic fingers of a cheap motel bed, and the sight of it turned my stomach sour. I turned my head to the side and puked the feeling away, but the combination of the sight and the sounds that Glenn-thing was making left me still queasy and hot-mouthed.

"Keep holding on," I said. I plugged the tiny television into the socket on the wall behind the shrine. "It won't be long now. Just keep holding that thing in there."

Glenn-thing responded with a moan that sounded like what I imagined people in hell being tortured for all eternity would sound like, but not just the cries of one poor soul. It was more like a thousand agony-filled wails rising up from the pit of despair combined into a single note of pain vibrating forth from Glenn-thing's vocal chords. I slammed the television on top of the shrine and pulled the knob out that turned it on, hoping we wouldn't be greeted by static and electric snow. It took a few seconds for the antiquated set to warm up, but when the screen finally kicked in it was just as I feared. The dreaded static that signified the lack of signal blanketed the screen and taunted me from behind the thin layer of glass.

"Fuck!" I exclaimed, spinning the dial only to find more of the same on every channel.

I smacked the side of the set several times trying to will the thing to work through violence but to no avail. That's when I grabbed the obscenely long antenna and began shifting it around back and forth in an attempt to catch some sort of free-flowing wavelength that would manifest itself on the screen as the information I was seeking. I wrenched the antenna up and over to the left as far as it would go, and the tip made contact with the metal of an exposed HVAC tube overhead. That must have given the antenna the signal boost it needed, because the static cleared away revealing an image of the president sitting at his desk in the middle of an address to the American people. I pumped my fist in the air to celebrate my victory over the television and quickly plopped down beside the moaning Glenn-thing, who was struggling to keep his quivering knees held together.

Even with the television screen being extremely small, and in black and white, I could still tell that the president was wearing a great deal of makeup. My guess was that bruise on his face given to him by Jim Charge's dick had only gotten worse.

"My fellow Americans," said the president in his signature cowboy-style draw. "Our great nation has come under attack today by one of the most brutal and vicious enemies we have come across in our illustrious history. This is a man who will stop at nothing to . . . take *charge* of all that we have for his own selfish gain."

I giggled at the uncomfortableness with which the president said the word *charge,* as I was sure I was the only one who truly understood what he meant.

"Our enemy, in this moment that I am speaking with you, has launched a nuclear missile at our great capital city of Washington, D.C. Rest assured your military have been using everything within their power to stop this missile and redirect it away from bringing harm to our country. However they have been met with . . . some resistance."

The camera cut away from the president to show choppy news footage of the missile flying through the sky. There was a tiny black outline of a bump on the missile that to anyone else watching would appear to be part of the weapon of mass destruction, but I knew better. The footage went on to show military men launching surface to air missiles at it, only to watch in disbelief as their target changed course by pulling up or rolling from side to side, completely evading the attempts to blow it out of the sky. It cut to another scene in which a squadron of F-16s had the missile completely surrounded until something shot out from the side of it and hit the nose of the lead plane. I was the only one who knew it was the powerful leg of Jim Charge delivering a bone crushing kick to the flimsy steel of the fighter plane. The F-16 was violently thrown off course and smashed into the plane beside it, which spun off into the plane on the other side, which then spun end over end backward taking out the final plane bringing up the rear. The clip cut away as the four planes were sent careening to Earth while each pilot ejected to parachute down on the heels of the wreckage.

I hugged my knees to my chest, unable to stop smiling as I watched my Number 1 ride a nuclear missile while thwarting any and all attempts to bring it down. They cut away from the footage of the crashing planes and back to the president at his desk. To say he looked pissed off would be quite the understatement.

"While I know this may look like the enemy has the better of us I assure you that is not the case," he continued solemnly. "Your president and your military have a plan in place that is guaranteed to bring this missile down before it has a chance to cause any further death or destruction."

The camera cut to a dramatically close shot of the president's face as he delivered the final line of his speech.

"With god as my witness," he growled, "I will bring down this missile and rip the dick off of our new enemy. This I promise you."

The president's face disappeared from the screen and was replaced by an old stock image of the American flag waving in the breeze as the national anthem played in the background. Glenn-thing released a slightly muffled cry that was followed by a pop and the distinct sound of a large quantity of liquid smacking against a flat, hard surface. I watched a puddle spread out from beneath the reclining Glenn-thing and felt it soak into my pants as it spread out across the floor. Glenn-thing's water had broken, and I didn't think he was going to be able to hold on much longer.

I looked back to the flag on the television screen and imagined it was replaced by the Charge Land flag that Jim had me make.

"Please hurry Jim," I said to the screen. "Please hurry."

Chapter Sixteen

While I had given up on second-guessing or wondering what Jim's plan was for this whole missile riding scenario I had to admit that I was starting to come unglued from the stress. After the president signed off I sat in the puddle of Glenn-thing's womb water, staring at the image of the flag, willing more information to be given from the antiquated television set. I spun the dial searching for another channel, but all I found was the same flag or static snow.

As much as I wanted to ignore the pain-filled groans of Glenn-thing their intensity had increased so much that I couldn't. I started to come to terms with the fact that Jim Charge might not make it back in time, or even worse not at all. He was riding through the sky on a nuclear missile after all, and even though he was Jim Charge he was still only human. Wasn't he? I got up and hurried over to the home decor section of the nearly destroyed department store and gathered a handful of towels that I determined were covered in the least amount of piss. I rushed back to Glenn-thing and dropped them by his side before heading back to the break room to retrieve some water. I found a pot that was mostly used for cooking employee lunches of Ramen and boiling water for instant coffee.

I filled the pot with water, placed it on the stove and turned the burner on high. I honestly wasn't sure what I was going to do with these things, but on every television show I'd seen where someone was going to give birth before they could get to a hospital they always told some bit character to go get towels and boiling water. The best that I could figure was that you put the pregnant woman's hand in the warm water so that she pissed herself thereby also expelling the baby from her womb in the process. I guess you used the towels to clean up the piss and possibly catch the baby with. I watched the water waiting for it to come to a boil when I heard Glenn-thing call out to me. Or at least attempt to.

"Yearghhh . . . the T.V. is ohhhhhhh . . . the missile is . . . ahhhhh fuck!"

The water was nowhere close to boiling, but it would have to do. I snatched it from the flame and sprinted back to Glenn-thing hoping against hope that I wouldn't arrive to find the baby Charge lying on the floor in a puddle of piss. Thankfully that was not the case, but what I did see made me drop the pot of lukewarm water and rush to turn up the television. Apparently the network received footage from a third party news team who had used high-powered satellite imaging to zoom in on the missile, revealing Jim Charge riding it through the air.

I paid no attention to what the newscaster was saying as they showed the footage because I was fixated on what Jim Charge was doing. I could clearly see that he still held the bobby pin I had brought him between his teeth while squeezing the boxes of cosmetics under each arm. Jim shifted the boxes from under his right arm over to where he held the rest under his left and plucked the bobby pin from his mouth. He worked the thin piece of metal between two of the steel plates that made up the missile's casing until one popped open. He ripped the piece of casing away letting it fly off behind him and began digging through the boxes, grabbing handfuls of blush, powder, lipsticks and eye shadow, shoving them all into the opening he had created.

He emptied the first box, let it fly off behind him like

the steel plate and then began stuffing similar contents from the next box into the missile. They cut away at this point back to the newscaster sitting stone-faced behind his desk.

"These are the startling images of the enemy riding atop his implement of death as it careens toward Washington. As far as we know all attempts to stop the missile from reaching its target have been thwarted, and it appears that we may have run out of time to try anything else."

The newscaster stopped here, put his hand to the tiny device in his ear and appeared to be listening intently.

"Ladies and gentlemen," he continued, "I am being told that the president is about to address the nation once again. We are now switching to his private feed streaming directly from the White House."

The picture cut quickly back to the desk that the president sat behind during his initial address, but he was not sitting behind it anymore. A moment later the president walked into the frame in front of his desk wearing a shiny black, skintight suit. An American flag was stitched just above his heart, and there was a metal ring around his collar that looked like a helmet could snap into it, similar to the way a spacesuit worked. Draped across his pitiful concave chest was a red, white and blue sash that said *President* in bold white lettering. The president walked in front of his desk, placed his hands behind his back and puffed his chest out. It was quite obvious by the lack of bulge in his crotch that his team of scientists hadn't attached his new dick yet.

He took a deep breath. "My fellow Americans, as I'm sure you know by now our attempts to bring the missile down have failed. That is why I have decided to take it upon myself, as your fearless leader, to stop it from reaching its target of Washington, D.C. We now know that our enemy is actually riding the missile to its destination Kamikaze-style, making him the most insane and evil threat we have ever faced."

Two Secret Service men stepped into frame behind the president and set a helmet and another piece of machinery onto his desk.

"Using a highly confidential and still experimental jetpack technology I, your courageous leader, will take to the sky and singlehandedly kill our new enemy. Once I have dispatched this nuisance, I will diffuse the missile and ride it safely and harmlessly to the ground."

One of the Secret Service men lifted the jetpack, and placed it onto the president's back where it snapped into place holding tight against his suit. The other agent handed the helmet to the president before they both walked off and out of frame.

"Rest assured people," he continued. "Your president will save the day. God bless America."

With that the President walked around his desk to the window behind it, threw it open and jumped out. As soon as he was clear of the glass the jetpack fired up, and the president flew off into the sky like a shot. His trajectory mirrored that of a bird with one wing falling to Earth, but a moment later he righted himself and headed straight up. The camera cut back to the newscaster who looked rather confused until he realized that he was on back on the air.

"Uhhh. Well . . ." he stumbled. "That was the president telling us he is using a prototype jetpack technology to fly into the sky, kill the man riding the missile and then diffuse it all on his own."

I could tell it was hard for the reporter to say this and keep a straight face.

"I'm being told we will be immediately switching to a feed of the president's encounter with the missile," he continued. "Let us all pray that he is successful."

The screen went to static for a moment before it cut to a wide shot of the president flying through the air at tremendous speed on a direct course for the missile.

Chapter Seventeen

"**I** can't! I can't! I just can't do it!" Glenn-thing screamed in my face as he did his best to hold Jim's son in the womb of the body his head had been attached to.

"You've got to!" I yelled back, slapping him several times in the face, hoping to distract him from wanting to push. "You saw what happened! Jim will be back any minute now, and his plan will be complete. You didn't hold on this long just to blow it now, did you? No you didn't, so hang the fuck on!"

Jim Charge's victory had been so beautiful, but with Glenn-thing screaming in agony I had little time to relish in it. After the news broadcast cut to the president flying toward the missile from the White House window I held my breath in anticipation as anxiety and fear began to overtake me. The president was heading right for the missile at what appeared to be a very high speed, but the missile wasn't diverting from its course to avoid him. I started to wonder if perhaps Jim had abandoned the missile during the president's speech, or worse had fallen off and crashed down to his death.

The camera zoomed to a tighter shot as the president got closer to the missile, and my fears were once again assuaged when I saw the unmistakable silhouette of Jim Charge standing up on the missile and jumping off. Jim managed to align his descent with the president's ascent and caught the jetpacked world leader in mid-air. The camera shot shook violently as it tried to zoom in closer to the tangled twosome as they wrapped each other up and began to plummet. It was obvious the two were struggling but the camera was shaking so badly that I couldn't tell what was happening. The camera operator pulled the shot back for a wider view just in time to show Jim Charge swing the president around in mid-air and launch him straight toward the tip of the missile. I didn't realize that he had taken the president's jetpack from him until his beefy silhouette shot off through the sky in the opposite direction of the nuke.

The camera pulled out further to show that the missile was directly over the White House when the president's ragdoll of a body made direct contact with it. There was an instant explosion but not like the kind I'd seen in stock footage of bombs being tested back in the 'Fifties or even what it looked like when Japan was bombed. There appeared to be a great deal of smoke generated by the explosion, but there didn't seem to be any of the fire that usually accompanies the smoke when a bomb explodes.

The cloud the bomb emitted grew larger and larger until it covered the entire White House and rolled off to each side, completely filling the tiny television screen until it looked like I was just watching static again. They cut back to the newscaster who was clearly terrified and made no attempt to hide it.

"Ladies and gentlemen," he said flustered, "we're not sure what has exactly happened here, but it appears that our president has been thrown into the missile, and that it has been detonated directly over the White House. This is not a test, and I'm sure that Washington, D.C., is being evacuated at this time, that is if there is even anyone left to evacuate. Please stay tuned for an update as soon as we . . . "

The newscaster stopped and put his hand to his earpiece again, listening intently to what was being said to him through it. His face turned from terror to confusion as he looked around the studio at the cameraman and director who were hearing the same thing.

"Is this right?" he asked to someone off-camera to his left. "It can't be, can it? Okay, okay, whatever you say."

The newscaster turned his attention back to the camera and once again addressed the viewers.

"Ladies and gentlemen, I have just received a report that this attack may not be what we initially thought. It seems we have made contact with our White House field reporter who is not only still alive but has vital information for us. Let's go live to him now, if you can believe it, from the White House."

The scene cut now to a shot that was completely filled with smoke. It took a moment to realize there was a person standing a few feet in front of the camera, waving something away from their face with one hand and putting the microphone that was in the other hand up to their mouth. Eventually I was able to make out facial features, and a few seconds later enough of the smoke had been cleared to see the reporter's face clearly. I couldn't believe what I was seeing. The reporter, a man who appeared to be in his mid- to late-forties, stood in front of the camera with a puzzled look on his face, a face that was completely covered in makeup.

The makeup wasn't applied in the skillful way that Jim Charge applied makeup to Glenn-thing, though. Everything was in the right place as far as lipstick, blush and eye shadow went. Only there was an implied harshness to the way it had been applied. The lipstick, that I could only guess was *Russian Red* since the television was black and white, looked like it was drawn more around the lips instead of on them, and the edges were smeared back all the way across his cheeks to his earlobes. The blush looked more like two circular chunks were blown out of his cheeks with a fifty-caliber machine gun and did nothing to extenuate his bone structure. The excess rouge smeared down his face making it look worn and ruddy. The makeup around his eyes looked like the thick black circles of death one might see on someone trying to dress up like a zombie for Halloween.

It looked like he had achieved the effect by standing in front of a cannon full of makeup and letting it shoot him in the face. The footage of Jim using the bobby pin to open the missile's casing so he could stuff in the cosmetics flashed through my mind, and I realized what Jim had done.

"Ladies and gentlemen," started the reporter, "I am standing on the White House lawn at ground zero, and while I seem to be unharmed it is still unclear what exactly is going on."

The smoke started to clear more from around the reporter, and I could see people staggering around in the shot behind him. They, too, had faces that looked like someone had fired a sawed-off full of makeup into as well.

"As far as this reporter can tell," he continued, "there doesn't appear to be any casualties, or at least none in my general vicinity. The strange thing is that it looks like everyone in the blast zone has had their faces covered in . . . makeup."

The reporter brought his hand to his face and wiped his cheek vigorously, but the makeup didn't even so much as smear. He turned around to acknowledge two people who had walked up to him.

"Behind me it appears to be the Secretary of State. Madame Secretary, may I have a comment on what just happened here."

The government official looked down at the microphone, confused, and then up to the reporter before she opened her mouth to speak, but I couldn't hear what she was saying. I thought that I was perhaps having a stroke as a loud whistling sound filled my ears until I looked over at Glenn-thing and could tell by his expression that he was hearing the same thing. The whistling grew louder and more intense as whatever was causing it got closer. I turned back to the images flickering across the black and white screen. The reporter, the Secretary of State and the man accompanying her had all been assaulted about the face in the same fashion causing them to take on the appearance of a roving band of zombie clowns.

The images disappeared from the screen as the whistling reached a fevered pitch and the ceiling crashed down around us. A moment later I realized that Glenn-thing and I were unscathed by the falling debris, and as the dust settled I saw the unmistakable outline of Jim Charge standing in front of us. He was dressed in an aqua-green, light cotton suit that mimicked the appearance of doctor scrubs. The ascot around his neck doubled as a facemask, and he pulled the handkerchief from his breast pocket, popped it open and tied it around his head to cover his hair. The most prominent accessory to this particular suit, however, was the red, white and blue sash the president had been wearing when he jetpacked through the window of the Oval Office. Glenn-thing moaned in delight at the sight of Jim Charge, knowing that his pain would soon be over.

"Jim," I said, standing up and brushing the dust off of me best I could, "your plan worked, didn't it? We won, didn't we?" I searched his face for a look of confirmation and was met with a subtle smile I could not interpret. "I went and got some towels. I started boiling water, but I . . ."

Jim Charge gently pushed me to the side and made a b-line for the wide open, propped up legs of Glenn-thing, whose convulsing vagina yearned to relax its hold. Jim grabbed Glenn-thing's knees, and pulled them apart as wide as they could go.

"Thank god I can finally start pushing," said Glenn-thing.

Before he could, however, Jim Charge reared back and thrust his hand elbow deep up into Glenn-thing's swollen snatch. The look of pain-fueled surprise took over his face and made me wonder if Jim had missed the baby and actually had a strangle hold on Glenn-thing's spine. Jim moved his hand around a bit until it landed on what he was looking for, and he then proceeded to yank the fruit of *his* loins from the *mutant* loins the baby had been grown in. Glenn-thing emitted a cry of pain so unique and terrifying that I hoped in my lifetime I would never have to experience even a quarter of the pain that made him make that sound.

Jim Charge struck a pose like that of a Viking warrior post-victory, holding up the head of his enemy for all to see, only instead of a head Jim held up his afterbirth-drenched son.

"Look, my son," said Jim Charge, holding the boy up triumphantly. "All you see in this store, as well as all the land that stretches out in every direction around it has been conquered by me in the Charge name that we now share."

I rarely become emotional over anything and count my fortitude in this as one of my strongest characteristics. It must have been the combination of everything that had happened over the past several hours coupled with seeing this first exchange between father and son that broke me down, because I started bawling. I do have to say it felt good to cry. It was the final emotional release I needed after putting a tremendous amount of pressure on myself to be the best Number 2 I could, and standing there seeing Jim wearing the president's sash and holding up the next in line to take up the Charge name made me realize it was all worthwhile.

"You will try hard in your lifetime to top the other Charge men who came before you, and it will be an uphill battle all the way, but you will go to your grave knowing that it was *your* father who bested you before you were even born. Now what do you have to say about that?"

While it wasn't the kind of speech you'd expect a father to give to his newborn son seconds after he'd yanked him from the womb, it was still quite beautiful in its own regard. Jim Charge lowered the baby to his eyelevel and studied his face. He did a double take, wiped the slimy remnants of Glenn-thing's cooch from the boy and looked at him again.

"Oh no," said Jim, his tone sounding suddenly distraught. "No, no, no this can't be! How did this happen?"

I was in front of Jim so all I could see was the frantic look on his face as he held the child up in front of him. Something dark gray started pushing out from the baby's skin, and after a moment I realized what was happening. He was growing his first suit. A second later he was completely clothed and clean of any trace of the birth slime he had been covered in.

"Oh god, no! Nooooooo!" Jim cried out in anguish as the suit fully formed around the boy.

"What is it Jim?" I demanded, instantly regretting my tone.

Jim slowly turned the baby around in his arms so that it was facing me. The first thing I noticed was the suit and how utterly unsophisticated and mediocre it was. I know the kid was just born, but I would expect a Charge man's style to be an inherent trait from birth. The suit on this baby was poorly made, ill-fitting and looked exactly like a suit from the discount rack of the department store. In fact it looked just like the kind of suits that Glenn used to wear. It was then I saw what had prompted Jim Charge's unpleasant reaction. The child looked exactly like Glenn.

I don't mean that in the family resemblance way either. The baby that Jim Charge held in his giant, shaking hands was the spitting image of Glenn, only all of his features had been transferred to a smaller space.

"What in the hell is that supposed to be?" I raised my voice quite louder than I would ever dream of doing while addressing Jim Charge, and I was suddenly so overwhelmed with disgust for what I was seeing and for my behavior that I turned my head to the side to puke. I heaved violently for a few moments before there was nothing left inside me, and I bent over with my hands on my knees to catch my breath.

"What's going on guys?" Glenn-thing's voice came from behind Jim where he'd been left to recover from the birthing. "What are you guys yelling about? Is there something wrong with the kid or what?"

Jim slowly turned the baby around so that he faced Glenn-thing.

"Ahhhh," said Glenn-thing, smiling. "He's a cute little devil, isn't he?"

The look on Jim's face hardened into an expression of cold hatred, and he gently set the baby on the floor at his feet while maintaining eye contact with a very confused Glenn-thing.

"What's wrong? Did something happen that I don't know about? Did the president end up ripping *your* dick off?"

Jim closed the gap between him and Glenn-thing in a flash, shedding the scrubs-style suit he was wearing in the process, which changed quickly back to a basic, yet elegant, black suit with a white shirt and a wide black tie. Before Glenn-thing could literally take half a breath, Jim Charge had grabbed him by the top of his head and ripped it from the body of Missy Cummings. Glenn-thing was now once again just Glenn's head. Jim was seething with anger and large veins began to pulse and shudder up and down the sides of his neck like earthworms doing the death dance on a hot sidewalk. He held Glenn's head out toward the baby and pointed with his other hand.

"What is the meaning of this . . . thing?"

"What? What thing?" He swung from the firm grip of

Jim's bulldozer of a fist as Glenn's head attempted to grasp what was happening. "And also, ouch! What the hell d'you rip my head off for again?"

"Did you and Missy Cooper engage in sexual relations very recently prior to my . . . impregnating of her?"

"Sexual what?"

"Answer me you pathetic excuse for a half-brained sub-human!"

"Well," sputtered Glenn's head, "if by sexual relations you mean me, Missy and my fake girlfriend that you killed earlier having wild monkey sex together in the break room on the reg, and as recent as two days ago, then yes. Yes, I had sexual relations with that woman."

I took a breath and in that moment time stood still as I saw the look of absolute heartbreak piled high with defeat take over Jim's face and change it into something I did not recognize. His black suit fell off changing into a red suit, then a brown suit and then a deep blue suit all in the matter of a few seconds just before he chucked Glenn's head halfway across the store. My Number 1 crashed to the floor next to the baby and sat Indian-style with his arms folded across his beefy chest. The ground shook from the force of him sitting and more dust and plaster hunks fell from the ceiling now damaged beyond repair.

Glenn's head clattered off the rubble in the distance and when all was silent I couldn't wait another moment to ask.

"Jim," I blurted out, trying to sound calm, "what is going on? Why does your son look exactly like . . . like Glenn?" I tried unsuccessfully to not make the end of my question sound like I was disgusted, but I honestly couldn't help it.

"Because," spat Jim back at me, "he's not *my* baby. He's *our* baby."

"He's . . . he's *our* baby?"

"Not mine and yours, you idiot. Mine and . . . that head."

"I don't understand."

"I don't know how I could have missed it!" Jim sounded like someone had EQ'd the confidence out of his voice.

"Missed what?"

"Glenn must have fertilized the egg in Missy's womb during their most recent sex romp, but then I flooded her works with Charge seed which took the fertilization process over from Glenn's weak spineless sperm. But something went wrong."

"Something went wrong? Seems a tad understated don't you think?"

The Charge baby with the head of Glenn sat up all his own and babbled nonsense at us while chewing the hanky he'd pulled from his jacket pocket.

"I was a load short," he said with a long low sigh.

"A load short? Is that a euphemism for something?"

"No, Number 2. I'm afraid it means exactly what it sounds like. If I had been able to pump just one more load into Missy's tainted baby-maker the takeover would have been complete, and this," he gestured toward the Glenn-headed child, "would never have happened."

Chapter Eighteen

Jim went on to tell me that he *had* actually fired the correct amount of loads from his horse-cock of a cock, but he'd wasted one in vain settling a bet between the two of them that he couldn't hit the jewelry counter on the other side of the store. He proved to her that he indeed could hit the counter, thereby winning the bet. This also explained why the entire area surrounding their lovemaking was covered in a sticky slime of goo. I wondered why the baby being part-Glenn made much of a difference, but I didn't dare ask the question out loud.

Don't get me wrong. The last thing I would want is to have my kid be half-Glenn, but if the whole point of what Jim did was to pre-out-do his son and leave a legacy that could never be surpassed, then mission accomplished. What did it matter if the kid was slightly tainted by a weaker sperm? Jim still accomplished what he set out to do, didn't he? The baby started getting fussy after Jim explained the load situation to me and demanded to be picked up. Jim Charge sighed heavily, stood up with the baby in his arms and sulked off towards the break room. I walked over to the tiny television to see if any other information was available regarding the makeup-filled nuke my Number 1 detonated over Washington.

The screen flickered with footage of people walking the streets of Washington like confused zombies, all with the same makeup blasted on their faces, and all seemingly wondering if they were even really still alive. The reporter talking over the footage didn't have any real information to offer except for predicting the imminent price gouging of makeup remover in D.C. and the surrounding areas. The camera cut back to the anchorman behind the desk who looked like he'd aged forty years during the span of the broadcast.

"Ladies and gentlemen," he said, "it is with a heavy heart that I bring you the news of what appears to be the only casualty of the entire attack. It has just been confirmed that our former president has been found in pieces scattered across the White House lawn. The only part of him that has not been located so far is his penis. If anyone has information on the whereabouts of this penis, please call your local authorities immediately. White House officials are asking that citizens check their gutter, bushes and other areas around their homes where the penis may have ended up."

"Oh man, Jim, they're actually looking for that dickless wonder's dick," I said, whirling around to the empty space behind me.

I forgot that Jim was off taking care of his baby now, and for a moment the thought that my entire relationship with my Number 1 was about to change stormed my brain and took it over. I dismissed the thought, not allowing myself to start worrying about that just yet. The anchorman continued to talk from the television behind me, and I turned back around to hear the rest of the story.

"I say our *former* president," continued the anchor, "not because he is now deceased, but because apparently it wouldn't matter even if he wasn't. I've been given an official proclamation which I have been instructed to read to you on the air right now."

I looked over my shoulder hoping to see Jim Charge coming back from the break room so he could see what was going on, but there was no one there. From the far side of the store I could hear the groaning of Glenn's head as he regained consciousness, but I ignored him and turned back to the television where the anchor was starting to read the announcement.

"People of the country formerly known as the United States of America," he began. "It is with great pleasure that I bring you this exciting news about the state of your country. I have killed your greedy, self-serving, piss-poor excuse for a president and am now your new commander-in-chief. Please keep in mind that I did not kill any other citizens, and the makeup you have been blasted with is just my way of leaving my mark. I assure you that it will wash off in a few weeks. My name is Jim Charge, and you will come to know me very well as I begin my reign over this fine land. That being said, from this point on this country will no longer be known as the United States of America but instead will now be called Charge Land."

A shiver of excitement ran up my spine and shook a huge smile free upon my face when the anchor said the words: Charge Land. Hearing the words also sent blood coursing through my penis resulting in quite an impressive erection. An erection that quickly wilted when I heard Glenn's head calling from across the store.

"Hello? Hello, can you guys hear me? What the hell happened to me? Where's my body, and why can't I see anything?"

I continued ignoring him and kept watching the TV.

"I understand that this news may be scary or confusing for most of you," the anchorman continued reading, "but let me assure you of one thing that is above all else. I am in Charge."

The anchorman placed the paper on his desk and looked back into the camera once again. "Well, that seems pretty straight forward, folks. Allow me to be the first among you to say, God bless Charge Land!"

The anchor then reached under his desk, pulled up a small wooden box and set it in front of him. He opened the box and removed several items that were obscured by the bottom of the tiny screen. When he picked one of the items up and opened it there was no mistaking that it was a compact, and he carefully studied himself in the small mirror while applying the cheap grocery store brand powder to his wrinkled pus. He then puckered up his thin, wrinkled lips while untwisting an equally generic brand of lipstick. I pushed the knob in on the television to turn it off and went to look for Jim.

Glenn's head's moans and cries for help were getting to be too much to ignore, so I followed the sound of his voice until I found the head way off in the far corner of the juniors department, wrapped up in a ball of rayon scarves.

"I can see," said Glenn's head as I untangled him from the mess of scarves. "Thank god I can see! Now what the hell happened to me? Didn't I have tits like half an hour ago?"

I refreshed Glenn's head on the recent events that had transpired, and it all came back to him. I explained the cross-fertilization that had occurred just as Jim had explained it to me, which resulted in the baby being part-Glenn and looking just like him. I also told him what I saw and heard on the television, and that as far as I could tell it appeared as though Jim Charge was indeed *in charge* of the country.

"Well," said Glenn's head, "where is Jim now? What's the next move, you know? I mean, what happens to us now?"

"That's what I intend to find out," I said as we entered the break room.

Sitting on the counter was the just-born Charge baby greedily sucking down a bottle he held by himself in his left hand, while he clutched a second full bottle in his right. In the light of the break room I could see just how cheap and tacky looking the suit the baby had grown was. It was pretty god-awful even on a baby, and the fact that the baby had Glenn's face didn't make it any better. On the small dining table in the middle of the room sat a large open suitcase filled with clothes. The lid slammed down on the suitcase to reveal Jim standing behind it.

"J-Jim," I stammered, "what is this? Where are you going?"

"Yeah," said Glenn's head from where he was perched in the crook of my arm. "Where are you . . . holy shit, you're right. That kid looks exactly like me!"

Chapter Nineteen

"Jim," I pleaded, "Jim, please don't go. Who cares about your kid having a little Glenn in him? I'm sure he'll grow out of it eventually. I bet when that kid hits puberty there won't be a trace of Glenn's ugly mug left on him. We won, for Christ's sake! *You* won! You set out to take over the entire free world in order to outdo your father and grandfather, while simultaneously making it impossible for your unborn child to ever be able to even think about outdoing you, ever, and you did it. You wanted to be the mightiest Charge man there was, and now that you've achieved it you're going to just walk away? What the hell was any of this even for?"

I didn't care that I was questioning my Number 1 anymore. I was reeling from the bomb that Jim had just dropped on me (no pun intended) and was in full on panic mode. I didn't want to believe it. I couldn't let myself believe it, but thinking this way didn't make it any less true. When I came in the break room with Glenn's head and saw Jim Charge closing his suitcase I figured I was about to receive directions to pack my own bag because we were finally leaving this shit-show of a department store. I was ready to spike Glenn's head in celebration as I imagined my Number 1 was about to tell me that we were relocating to a giant mansion in a top secret location to rule his new land in top of the line comfort and style.

What I didn't expect was for Jim Charge to tell me that he was taking the baby and leaving, *and* that neither Glenn's head nor myself were coming with him. Of course I wouldn't expect Glenn's head to go anywhere with us, but it was hard to grasp that I wouldn't be going either which is what set off my rambling and disrespectful rant.

"Look Number 2," said Jim Charge in a flat and emotionless tone, "I know this isn't the ideal situation that you may have expected, but I don't expect you to understand the Charge way."

"The Charge way?" I was still ranting along with a full head of steam, only now I was fighting back tears. "What does that even mean? You did everything you said you would do. *We* did everything we were supposed to! What is there for me to not understand?"

Jim stepped out from behind the table into the light, and I saw his makeup was different again. I must have been too worked up to notice it earlier, or it very well could have changed before my eyes without me noticing. Either way the fit I was throwing made me oblivious of the change until now. The deep red rouge that had been so elegantly brushed across Jim's sharp-lined features in long, perfect strokes was now gathered up into tightly concentrated circles of red that bloomed from the highest part of his cheeks just close enough to his eyes to walk the line between close and too close.

The edges of the blush-blooms broke up evenly into expertly stippled tiny red specks deceptively used to draw your eye down to his lips. They were painted a deep shade of ruby that I was unable to fully appreciate in the tragically ultra-violet lit break room. Circling each of his eyes was a simple clean thin, black line. They were not painted with shadow for the first time that I'd ever seen, which I thought was an odd choice for Jim. Astoundingly though, even this was a look that softened into to the perfectly blended background of base and concealer on the great Jim Charge.

"It doesn't count," he said simply. Jim was clearly not affected by my outburst. Either that or he was humoring me.

"Doesn't count?"

"Yes." The word fell like a dry lump of shit from his mouth. "It doesn't count. None of this counts. There are rules, Number 2. Rules that need to be followed very strictly for no reason other than that's how it has always been. There have been no previous exceptions, and there will be none now. This isn't a special case because there are no special cases. The rules forbid it."

"Rules? What rules?"

"*The* rules!" roared Jim, moving his face to within inches of mine. "Rules that must be followed because they always have been. Rules, that when followed, allow for what I . . . what we have done to count. Much like the rules you have placed upon yourself to be a great Number 2, the rules that you've followed so blindly in your pursuit of greatness, the rules I follow must be to the T. The smallest infraction, and I mean *smallest* negates the entire effort. I'll have to try again, but I won't get the chance for quite a while now."

Jim Charge softened his tone and moved his face away from mine as he finished his last sentence. Seeing this change in Jim took some of the wind out of my sails, but I wasn't through pleading.

"Okay," I said, "so there was a minor fuck up and a rule was broken. We don't have to start over, do we? Can't you just find another woman to impregnate, attach Glenn's head to and move on? We'll just call this one a mulligan, ditch the . . . uh . . . impure kid and make another one. I can go drop him off on the steps of the fire station while you find a new special lady to . . . couple with."

"I'd be okay with that," said Glenn's head. I had forgotten I was still holding him until he spoke. "Maybe this time you can find a chick with bigger cans, you know? I'm just saying it would make the whole experience worth my while."

The baby sitting on the counter sucked the last drops from the second bottle and chucked it at Glenn's head, hitting him smack-dab in between the eyes. Jim Charge picked his son up, pulled a full bottle from his jacket pocket and shoved the nipple in the child's waiting mouth. He then walked back over to the table and secured the clasps on his suitcase making sure it was closed tight.

"Yes, Number 2," he said, "in theory that is exactly what we should do, and may be exactly what I *do* do, but not yet. Probably not for a long time."

I opened my mouth to reply, but no sound came out as I realized my relationship with Jim Charge was ending, and I could see a sadness in his darkly lined eyes that told me he was thinking the same thing. The thick silence that hung between us was sliced in two when Glenn's head finally spoke up again.

"Okay, okay," he said. "The new chick doesn't necessarily have to have huge tits. I'm willing to sacrifice that for the greater good of . . . whatever this whole thing is about."

While it was crudely put and entirely self-serving, I still appreciated Glenn's head's attempt at trying to convince Jim Charge to stay. The Charge baby finished the new bottle Jim had given him and, as if on cue, chucked it at Glenn's head again hitting him in nose this time.

"Come on man," groaned Glenn's head. "The first time was kind of cute, but that one hurt."

The baby laughed and clapped his hands, clearly pleased with his aim. Jim produced another bottle from the same jacket pocket, and the baby quickly snatched it from his hand and began suckling happily.

"How long?" I asked, not breaking eye contact with Jim. "How long is a *long* time?"

"That really all depends," he said, now lightly bouncing the baby in his arms. "I made my attempt at outdoing the Charge men who came before me while simultaneously trying to outdo my unborn offspring before he even had a chance, so now he gets one."

"He gets one, what?"

"He gets a chance," said Jim, nodding toward the child whose head was nuzzled against his shoulder. "According to the rules I don't get another chance to try and outdo any member of the Charge lineage until after my son has had his chance."

"Are you saying that we have to wait until this kid grows up and tries to get one over on you before we can even try to do anything like . . . this again?"

"Possibly," said Jim, maintaining a cool evenness in his tone. "It might happen sooner than that, though. My great-great-great grandpa Charge made an attempt to outdo his father when he was two years old, and he succeeded, too. It was a simpler time back then, and he managed to seduce his father's secretary using his baby cuteness, Charge charm and an abnormally large dick. I know it sounds weird, but he was very mature for his age, and like I said, it was a . . . simpler time. He tricked her into giving him access to the company's documents and accounts, and he changed them all to be in his name. The next day when his father came to work he learned that he had been terminated, and that his baby son had pulled the company out from under him while banging his secretary and now ex-lover. The two were married later that year. He was . . . a great man."

"So, that chick fucked a baby?" asked Glenn's head.

"Yes she did," answered Jim, "but like I said they were eventually married, so it was all fine."

"Are you saying that if this baby fucks your secretary, or whatever the equivalent to that would be for you, then we . . . I mean *you* can try to top the Charge men again?" I asked. "I mean, if that's allowed by the rules."

"Not exactly," said Jim, "but possibly. You see, in the case of my great-great-great grandpa, he succeeded in his attempt to outdo his father thereby making him the dominant Charge. Once a Charge father is outdone by his son he is no longer permitted to participate in the outdoing of other Charge men. If that weren't a rule then we'd all be trying to outdo each other our entire lives until it eventually consumed our existence. When my son does make his attempt, which is inevitable, he would have to fail for me to have a second chance to once again attempt to outdo him and both my father and grandfather."

The last bit of hope I had made a mass evacuation, and I felt like a deflated balloon whose air was released from a hole in my heart. I stopped fighting back my tears and hung my head letting them flow freely.

"I see," I said, not making eye contact with Jim anymore. "So if your son fails to outdo you at whatever point in his life he decides to try, then I guess you'll go take the country from whatever power-hungry, war-mongering, dickless president who happens to be running it at that time?"

"No," said Jim.

He placed the milk-drunk, sleepy baby on top of his suitcase and the boy burped like a three hundred pound truck driver before curling up, jamming a thumb into his mouth and passing out. Jim walked across the room to where I stood holding Glenn's head, softly sobbing. He gently placed his finger on my chin and raised my head so I that I had to look back into the eyes I had hoped I'd never have to say goodbye to.

"I'll have to take it . . . from you."

With that Jim Charge removed the presidential sash from his chest, placed onto mine and lightly kissed me on the cheek.

Chapter Twenty

I didn't think I'd be able to adapt to Jim being gone and becoming a Number 1 as quickly as I did, but the transition happened seamlessly. I reported to the White House, and just as Jim said, they were expecting me. Everything was in order for me to take over as leader of the free world, and even stranger, everyone seemed to be pretty okay with it.

More than that, people saw my overtaking the country as a breath of fresh air compared to the old hillbilly who held the position prior to me. A lot of the people in D.C. even decided to keep their post-attack look by continuing to wear makeup daily in the same style it was applied to their faces from the nuke. The more extreme die-hards even had their makeup tattooed on them permanently. It was quite an achievement that I know Jim Charge would have especially enjoyed.

When Jim Charge picked up his suitcase in one arm and that hideous looking Glenn-faced baby in the other and walked out of that department store, I truly believed my life's purpose walked out with him. I almost didn't even go to Washington as Jim had instructed me to do because I felt more like lying in the rubble of the destroyed makeup-counter-turned-small-country and drown myself in a shallow puddle of piss. It was Glenn's head that convinced me to at least go see what it was like and if I still felt like dying I could jump from the top of the Washington Monument. He promised he wouldn't try to talk me out of it.

Another surprise that Jim arranged was declaring Glenn's head my vice president making him my Number 2 by default. Needless to say I wasn't too jazzed to receive this news but a note that was left for me on the desk of the Oval Office imbued me with the confidence I needed.

My dearest Number 2,
From the moment I saw you I knew that you would never become the great Number 2 you so desperately aspire to be. You over-analyze everything and ask far too many questions regarding the actions and decisions of me, your Number 1. It is because of these same things, however, that I knew you were destined to be a great Number 1. This is why I put you in charge of the country, but enjoy it while it lasts because one day I will come to take Charge Land back. Until then, I look forward to meeting the worthy opponent that I know you will become.
Love,
Jim Charge

P.S.
Don't be so hard on your new Number 2. He could end up being your greatest asset one day.

"Hey," said Glenn's head, resting on his vice presidential pillow that sat atop a chair that used to belong to Abe Lincoln. "Is that a note from Jim? What's it say? Did he mention anything about me?"

"Shut the fuck up, Glenn," I said, crumbling the note into a ball at tossing it across the Oval Office, hitting him right in the forehead. "Just shut the fuck up."

THE END

About the Author

John Wayne lives in Houston, TX, where he whiles away the days by writing ridiculous stories and slinging lattes for a bunch of jerks. When he's not doing that, he's touring with his bands: johnwayneisdead and Letters to Voltron. He also writes and illustrates his own zine, *The Afterlife Adventures of johnwayneisdead.*

Made in the USA
Middletown, DE
12 September 2019